# J. T. EDSON'S FLOATING OUTFIT

The toughest bunch of Rebels that ever lost a war, they fought for the South, and then for Texas, as the legendary Floating Outfit of "Ole Devil" Hardin's O.D. Connected ranch.

MARK COUNTER was the best-dressed man in the West: always dressed fit-to-kill. BELLE BOYD was as deadly as she was beautiful, with a "Manhattan" model Colt tucked under her long skirts. THE YSABEL KID was Comanche fast and Texas tough. And the most famous of them all was DUSTY FOG, the ex-cavalryman known as the Rio Hondo Gun Wizard.

J. T. Edson has captured all the excitement and adventure of the raw frontier in this magnificent Western series. Turn the page for a complete list of Berkley Floating Outfit titles.

A FLOATING OUTFIT STORY

# J.T. Edson

## A TOWN CALLED YELLOWDOG

BERKLEY BOOKS, NEW YORK

Originally published in Great Britain by Brown Watson Ltd.

This Berkley book contains the complete
text of the original edition.
It has been completely reset in a typeface
designed for easy reading, and was printed
from new film.

A TOWN CALLED YELLOWDOG

A Berkley Book / published by arrangement with
Transworld Publishers, Ltd.

PRINTING HISTORY
Corgi edition published 1968
Berkley edition / October 1981
Second printing / December 1983

ISBN: 0-425-06577-4

A BERKLEY BOOK ® TM 757,375
Berkley Books are published by The Berkley Publishing Group,
200 Madison Avenue, New York, New York 10016.
The name "BERKLEY" and the stylized "B" with design
are trademarks belonging to Berkley Publishing Corporation.
PRINTED IN THE UNITED STATES OF AMERICA

# A TOWN CALLED
# YELLOWDOG

## CHAPTER ONE

## The Scent of Fear

"You are about to enter MOONDOG, a quiet, friendly town. Enjoy your stay."

Riding his big *sabino* past the old scrub oak, Danny Fog read the words on a sign nailed to the gnarled trunk. Despite the welcome extended by the citizens of Moondog, San Augustino County, Texas, he wondered if he might be making a bad error in tactics. One man, even a Texas Ranger, had limitations. There were things he could not, should not even, try to do alone.

Unfortunately no other help had been available and the news from Moondog demanded an immediate investigation. Maybe the first letter received from the town had been a mite exaggerated, folks tended to multiply their troubles when writing to ask for assistance from the Texas Rangers. Yet it held a note of authenticity strong enough to make Danny's commanding officer, Captain Jules Murat, dispatch two good men to investigate. That had been three weeks ago, and no word came from the two Rangers; which surprised nobody at Company G's headquarters, for the wearers of the star-in-the-circle badge did not go in for sending reports when on a chore. However, a second letter, in the same neat handwriting as the first, reached Headquarters; a hot, angry letter demanding to know why the first request for assistance had been ignored.

Only two Rangers were present on the arrival of the letter, and the second still used crutches as a result of an outlaw's bullet. Captain Murat had taken a well-earned furlough and every other man rode scattered over their enormous jurisdictional area working on some case or other. So Danny made a decision. The two men sent in answer to the first request had had much experience in their work. By the end of three weeks they ought to have made their presence felt in the town. If they had not, then somebody must go and learn why.

Taking the precaution of sending a long telegraph message to Murat, Danny rode from headquarters in the direction of Moondog. Even if his two friends still worked undercover, he might be able to help them by bringing another unsuspected factor into the game they found themselves playing.

Moondog was a small town, no different in appearance and lay-out from a hundred such towns Danny had seen across the Texas plains. Most of the town's businesses lay along the straggled main street and in the homes of the citizens scattered in the background. Nothing out of the ordinary; no fine large houses, only wood or adobe cabins. However, one thing caught Danny's eye, a most unusual sight in Texas at that time. Not one of the men he saw in the streets wore a gun. Of course all appeared to be town dwellers, but even so, a man without a gun was a rare sight in the Lone Star State.

All the time as he rode, Danny was conscious of eyes studying him. He did not fear detection, for a Texas Ranger carried his badge of authority concealed and nothing about his dress or appearance set him apart from any of the thousands of young men following the cattle trade in the state that grew out of hide and horn. A low-crowned, wide-brimmed J. B. Stetson hat of Texas style sat on his curly, dusty blond head and threw a shadow on his handsome, intelligent, tanned face. Tight-rolled and knotted at his throat, a green bandana trailed long ends over his blue flannel shirt. He wore his levis pants cowhand fashion, outside his high-heeled, fancy-stitched boots and with the cuffs turned back. Maybe not every cowhand wore a gunbelt with matched staghorn butted 1860 Army Colts in fast-draw holsters, but in those days of percussion-fired hand-guns enough carried a spare weapon at the waist for a two-gun toter to be no novelty. Nor did the method of wearing the guns look out of the ordinary—the butt of the right side Colt pointed to the rear, that on the left turned forward to be available to either hand—for it was common enough among men who learned to shoot only with the right hand, yet wished to have a reserve weapon available. He rode a double-girthed, low-horned saddle of conventional pattern, rope strapped to the horn, Winchester Model '66 rifle booted at the left side and butt pointing to the rear, bedroll fixed to the cantle. While the *sabino*, a light red roan with a pure white belly, looked a fine animal, it bore a large brand as complicated as a skillet of snakes, and came from below the Mexican border, so gave no clue as to his identity. Tough and competent as he might look, nobody could say from his appearance that he rode as a member of the finest law enforcement organization in the world.

Although Danny studied the few horses tethered at hitching rails along the street, he saw no sign of his two friends' mounts. Ahead lay the open doors of Bescaby's Livery Barn, the name of the owner painted proudly and decoratively above its door. Danny noticed that much of the town's signwork bore the same decorative touch, an unusual thing in Texas at that time. In particular, he observed the front of the Blue Bull Saloon. While the building itself was not impressive, being a one-storey adobe structure, its sign sure caught the eye. Standing rampant in the position Danny knew all too well, an exceptional likeness of a longhorn bull glared its defiance at the world. However, one never saw a bull of such a bright shade of blue.

"Always heard artists were different from folks, old hoss," he remarked with a grin. "Looks like I heard true."

Instead of calling in at the saloon and satisfying his curiosity about the unusual colouration of the bull, Danny continued on down Main Street in the direction of the livery barn. He wanted to make contact with the other two Rangers as soon as possible, and figured the livery barn would be a good place to make a start. Livery barn owners ran barbers a good second when it came to spreading gossip and handing out news, maybe even licked the barbers for a lawman's purposes, for they saw more comings and goings than did their shop-bound rivals.

The doors of the Blue Bull opened and a tall young man stepped out, staring with envious eyes at Danny's big *sabino*. While the young man wore a dress of a range-country dandy, he did not have the look of a hard-working cowhand. Few cowhands spent so little time out of the elements that their faces retained the pallor sported by the slim young man. A fancy Navy Colt, with what looked like solid silver Tiffany grips, hung in the young man's fast-draw holster and his right hand hovered by it. His face, handsome in a fashion, had sullen, sneering lips and bore a thinly hidden hint of real cruelty. To a student of human beings, the young man appeared spoiled, pampered, weak-willed, arrogant and vicious. Such a combination out West meant either he could handle a gun real well, or was backed by somebody who was capable in *pistolero* matters. After watching Danny ride by, the young man turned and spoke to somebody inside the saloon, then swung his gaze once more to the *sabino*.

Not knowing the interest his horse had caused, Danny rode up to the double doors of the barn, swung from the saddle and entered. Only a few of the stalls had occupants and none of the horses present belonged to Danny's friends. However, he did not doubt the barn offered accommodation in a corral at the rear of the building and so he decided to look there after settling the *sabino* comfortably.

"Help you, mister?" asked a voice as he led the horse towards an empty stall.

Turning, Danny looked at the medium-sized, stocky, grey-haired man who came towards him. "Reckon so," he agreed. "I want to put up my horse for a spell."

"Sure thing," the man said, showing less eagerness

than one might expect from the owner of a business addressing a potential customer. "You working around these parts?"

"Nope," answered Danny, and caught a faint glimmer of a change in the man's expression, but it went before he could read it and a watchful blank look replaced it. "Anybody hiring up this way?"

"You could maybe ask Miss Howkins. She runs the Lazy H."

"She the only one doing any hiring?"

Again the flicker of something and once more the blank veil came down. Clearly the man meant to watch every word he said. It all fitted in with the claims made by the writer of the unsigned letter which brought the Rangers to Moondog.

"She runs the only spread around here," the man told him. "But I——"

The words died away as shadows fell across the room, stretching from the front doors. Slowly Danny swung on his heel, making like he examined the *sabino's* saddle, but looking towards the door. A glance at the livery barn owner gave Danny a shock. Fear etched itself on the man's face as he looked at the trio of shapes in the doorway. Yet Danny could see no cause for such fear. True, the two flank men bore all the signs of being professional hard-cases, hired bullies who sold their guns or muscles to the highest bidder, yet neither struck Danny as being anything exceptional. Nor, despite the fancy gun and fast-draw holster, did the slim young man. Danny knew most of the real fast men in Texas and could read the signs. No matter what kind of gun that slim, mean-faced cuss toted, he did not belong to the magic-handed group known as the top men of the lightning fast draw fraternity.

Without as much as a glance at the livery barn's owner, the slim young man walked forward. He came to a halt at Danny's side and looked the *sabino* over from head to tail.

"Nice horse, cowboy," he replied. "How much do you want for it?"

"It's not for sale," Danny replied.

"Reckon you don't know who I am, so I'll overlook that until you've been told," the young man hissed. "Tell him who I am, Bescaby."

"That's Stella Howkins' brot——," the owner began.

Swinging on his heel, the young man lashed out his hand, driving a bunched fist to Bescaby's belly. Much to Danny's amazement, the owner went back a couple of steps, clutched at his stomach, but made no attempt to defend himself. Howkins jumped forward, gripping Bescaby by the front of his vest and hauling him erect. At the door, the two hard-cases dropped their hands towards gun butts and grinned in Danny's direction, as if taunting him, daring him to object. While not afraid, Danny made no move to intervene. Way he saw it, Bescaby out-weighed Howkins and ought to be strong enough to handle the slim, pallid-faced young man, so Danny did not feel called upon to take a hand.

"Who am I?" gritted Howkins. "When I ask you that, don't say I'm anybody's brother." He shook Bescaby savagely, although the man ought to have resisted the move with no great trouble. "You hear me, Bescaby?"

Bescaby ran the tip of his tongue across his lips. "I—I hear you——"

"You hear me, *what*?"

"I—I hear you, Mr. Howkins."

"That's better!" Howkins snarled and released his hold. "And so you don't forget next time——"

Again Howkins' hand lashed out, the knuckles smashing into Bescaby's cheek and staggering the man a couple of paces. Catching his balance, Bescaby threw a glance at the two grinning gunmen, then raised a hand to the corner of his mouth. He looked down at the red smear of blood on his hand but said nothing.

Ignoring Bescaby, as if the man did not exist, Howkins turned once more to Danny.

"Now you know who I am," he said. "How much for the horse?"

"The answer's still the same."

Howkins stared as if he could not believe his ears. Then a low hiss of fury left his lips and his face darkened with anger. Stepping forward, Howkins lashed out his fist, aiming it at Danny's face. Faced by the young man, Danny felt even more puzzled why Bescaby allowed Howkins to rough-handle him. Certainly fear of Howkins' fistic powers could not have brought the meek acceptance, for the blow came slowly and telegraphed.

And this time Howkins struck at a man who learned self-defence from the masters of the ancient art of rough-house brawling.

Up came Danny's hands, catching Howkins' wrist as it drove forward. There were a number of ways in which Danny might have handled the attempted attack, all highly effective and very painful for the recipient, but he had the two hard-cases' presence to consider. Danny knew he must handle Howkins in such manner that he could also protect himself from the slim man's bodyguards.

A look of shock came to Howkins' face as he realized that Danny did not aim to stand and be hit. Much the same expression crossed the two hard-cases' features and for a vital moment they hesitated, unable to make their thoughts work in the face of such an unusual happening. Then thought and realization came—a good five seconds too late.

On catching Howkins' wrist, Danny twisted it downwards and behind the other's back. He expected some resistance from Howkins, but found the arm he held to be puny and weak. A squeal of rage and pain left Howkins' lips as his arm went up behind him. Pain held him motionless except for his voice.

The two hard-cases started to move forward, hands dropping again to their guns. Releasing the trapped wrist with his right hand and finding no difficulty in holding Howkins with the left, Danny drew his off-side Colt. He cocked the weapon as he brought it up, thrusting the barrel under Howkins' chin, gouging the muzzle in painfully.

"Hold it!" he ordered.

Always a fair judge of character, Danny figured this to be the best method of handling the situation. Without danger to himself, Howkins might have ordered the two men to make a play, gambling their lives in the hope that they downed Danny before he got them both. Such a gamble could have come off, for while he might drop one, the other would surely get him. Only with the gun under Howkins' chin such an order was certain to end with the young man dead.

A series of hand-claps sounded from the doors of the building and a feminine voice said: "Neatly done, cowboy. Now let him go!"

Without offering to obey the order—for order it had been—or give up his advantage, Danny turned his eyes towards the two men and a woman who stood just outside the barn's front doors. One quick glance showed Danny his wisdom in refusing to obey the order.

Take that jasper standing at the right of the woman, there stood a fair man with a gun. Maybe not top-grade stock, but still fast enough to make Danny regret any mistake in tactics. Tall, well-built, dandy-dressed and with right hand hovering the butt of one of his brace of low-tied Remington Army revolvers, that man spelled trouble to eyes which knew the West.

A slight frown creased Danny's brow as he looked towards the other man. Despite a neat brown beard, Danny recognized the man. Until a couple of months back Wally Greenwood had been a member of Company G. Then ugly rumours began to come in, tales of a Ranger who used his badge to extort money from saloon and brothel keepers. Captain Murat investigated but found no certain proof, which explained why Greenwood stayed alive and free. Although unable to prove anything, Murat discharged Greenwood as unsuitable for Ranger duties. From all appearances, the ex-Ranger had done well for himself. He wore expensive clothing and belted a low hanging Army Colt and, like his colleague, kept his hand close to it. Recognition was mutual as Greenwood's eyes met Danny's and a mocking sneer flickered across the ex-Ranger's face.

Ignoring Greenwood after one glance, Danny gave the woman a long, searching scrutiny. She stood maybe five foot eight, with a slim, but mature build, that a costly, travel-stained, frilly-busted blouse and a doe-skin divided skirt could not hide. A. J. B. Stetson hat rode on the back of her shoulder long, honey-blonde hair. While one could not say she was beautiful, her face had strength but an imperious coldness killed any charm it might possess. She stood slightly ahead of the two men, a riding quirt tapping her leg impatiently.

Howkins struggled impotently against Danny's grip, but froze as the cold nose of the Colt gouged deeper into his flesh.

"Reckon we'll just leave things stand the way they are, ma'am," Danny stated. 'And you just stand easy, *hombre*."

"Get him off me, Wigg, Greenwood!" Howkins screeched.

"They can try," Danny admitted. "Might even get me—but they'll have to scrape your brains off the ceiling when they get through with me."

Which was the simple gospel truth. No matter how the men managed to shoot Danny, he would let the held-back hammer of his Colt fall to ignite the percussion cap, fire the charge and propel a bullet up through Howkins' chin. At that range the bullet had more than sufficient power to drive through the top of Howkins' head and spray his brains across the ceiling.

At that moment Danny happened to glance at Bescaby. Never had he seen such terror as that shown on the barn owner's face. Danny could almost scent the smell of fear as Bescaby stared at the scene before him. If the Howkins family affected every citizen of Moon-dog in the same manner, then Danny figured it to be high time the Rangers made a thorough investigation.

"That feller jumped your brother for no cause at all, Miss Howkins," yelled one of the hard-cases.

"And you're a liar," she replied calmly. "I saw the whole thing. Get the hell out of here, both of you."

The two men turned and slunk out of the room with the attitude of a whipped cur expecting a kick in passing.

Once more Howkins struggled against Danny's grip, but with no more success than the cottontail in the grip of a big rattlesnake. "I only tried to buy his horse, Stella!" he yelped.

"Only I don't take to getting a hit in the mouth as boot for the deal," Danny put in.

"Release my brother," Stella Howkins said.

"And how about those two jaspers with you?" countered Danny.

"They won't make a move."

"They'd best not make one," Danny warned, releasing and shoving aside his captive. He retained the Colt in his right hand, an advantage that no amount of speed the two men might be capable of could off-set.

Staggering forward, Howkins let out a keening snarl of rage. He skidded to a halt and turned, a hand reaching towards his gun. Instantly his sister stepped forward, caught his arm and swung him to face her.

"Don't be dramatic, Harry," she purred—a sound as menacing as the hideous warning of a she-cougar guarding its cubs. "Go down to the saloon, I'll buy the horse for you."

Watching Stella Howkins' face, Danny saw why the men obeyed. Never had he seen such ruthless power, certainly not on any woman of his acquaintance. Clearly Stella Howkins had a will of iron and it would go badly with anybody who crossed her. Not a comforting thought to Danny as he aimed to do more than cross her, he aimed to stand there and flat refuse something she requested.

Throwing a malevolent scowl at Danny, Howkins turned and slouched out of the barn. Stella watched her brother go, gave a sorrowful head-shake and then swung back to face Danny.

"All right, cowboy," she said. "How much do you want for the horse?"

"Like I told your brother, ma'am," Danny replied. "It's not for sale."

A slight frown creased Stella's brow, drawing her eyes together and making her look mean as hell. From the little he had seen of her, Danny reckoned Stella could raise more anger with a little frown than most folks were capable of if they gave out a whole belly-full of cursing.

'I'll give you a hundred dollars and the pick of the Lazy H remuda."

"That's a tempting offer, ma'am. Only I've got kind of attached to that old *sabino* and sure wouldn't want to part with it."

Stella glanced at the gun Danny still held, then turned her eyes to the men flanking her. At any moment she would give them an order. Danny knew that for a fact, knew she would not allow the drawn gun to hold her back. So it appeared, did Greenwood. A momentary flicker of worry crossed the ex-Ranger's face. Having served in the same company as Danny, Greenwood knew the other's ability at handling a gun. Danny might not be real fast, it took him a good second to draw, and one needed half that speed to be reckoned fast, but he could call his shots with accuracy. Given an even start, Greenwood reckoned he and Wigg could take the Ranger and both come out of it alive; but not when Danny held a cocked revolver already in his hand.

"A Ranger needs a good hoss, Miss Howkins," Greenwood said.

## CHAPTER TWO

## He Knows Why I Hit Him

"A Ranger?" asked Stella, throwing a meaning glance at Wigg. "Are you a Texas Ranger?" she went on, turning her eyes once more to Danny.

"He for sure is," Greenwood answered. "That there's Danny Fog, the feller who got the bunch of *Comancheros* run by Choya Santoval, and bust up the cow thieves in Caspar County."*

"I see," she said, walking forward.

"Yes sir, Miss Howkins," Greenwood continued, watching Danny with mocking eyes as he followed the woman forward. "That there's Danny Fog, Dusty Fog's kid brother."

An annoyed glint came into Danny's eyes at the other man's last four words. Not that Danny felt ashamed of his relationship to the Rio Hondo gun wizard, but he figured his work as a Ranger entitled him to be a separate identity and not 'Dusty Fog's kid brother.' Nor was his dislike for Greenwood, the antipathy every honest lawman felt when confronted by a dishonest peace officer—even after the dishonest one's discharge—lessened by the way the man exposed him as a Texas Ranger. Again Danny felt no shame at being a member of the Rangers, but his work would be a damned sight harder now that people knew of his connections with the law.

"My offer is still open to you, Ranger Fog," Stella

* Told in THE COW THIEVES

**13**

said. "Please put that gun away, you don't need it now."

That figured. No man would deliberately make trouble with a Ranger unless he had a very good cause.

Spinning on his trigger-finger, Danny's Colt went back into leather. Then his right hand bunched into a fist and shot forward. Driven by powerful muscles, thrown in a manner taught by a man known for his fighting skill, the fist smashed into the side of Greenwood's jaw, spun him round twice and sent him crashing to the floor.

Apparently Danny's action in holstering his Colt had lulled the other's suspicions. Not only Greenwood was taken by surprise, Wigg hesitated just a moment too long. Even as his right fist smashed into Greenwood, Danny's left hand turned palm out and drew the nearside Colt in a cavalry-twist motion. By the time Wigg's brain sent an order, his move froze under the persuasive muzzle of Danny's fresh-drawn Colt. With fingers hovering a scant two inches from the right side Remington's butt, Wigg glanced at Stella for guidance.

Stella looked down at the dazed, sprawled-out Greenwood, then raised her eyes towards Danny. "Why did you do that?" she asked.

"Try asking him, ma'am," Danny replied keeping his attention on Wigg.

"Would he know?" she inquired.

"He knows why I hit him," Danny confirmed.

"I'd like *you* to explain."

"Greenwood rode as a Ranger. He knows why we don't show our badges."

"I see."

"Don't be *loco*, Wally!" Wigg shouted as the other sat up shaking his head, snarling curses and reaching towards his hip.

Then Greenwood's head cleared enough for him to think constructively. What he saw warned him that the Ranger held all the best cards in the game.

"Greenwood was only being helpful," Stella pointed out.

"Depends, ma'am," Danny answered.

"What on?"

"Who he was helping."

A faint smile came to the woman's lips, yet did not reach her eyes; they studied Danny in a calculating manner. Once before he had seen a woman examine him in the same manner; when Ella Watson, organizer of the Caspar County cow thieves first saw him, and not knowing him to be a Ranger, wondered if he would make a useful addition to her outfit.

"Greenwood might not like it," she pointed out.

"He can get up on his hind legs and tell me about it."

"There's that to it," Stella purred.

Slowly Greenwood climbed to his feet. He looked to Wigg for support and caught the almost imperceptible head-shake Stella gave the other man. On seeing his employer's signal, Wigg relaxed and clearly showed he did not intend to back Greenwood's play.

Watching Danny's Colt go back into its holster, Greenwood became conscious of four sets of eyes studying him. He knew Stella Howkins wanted to see how he handled the matter; which raised a point. Greenwood himself did not know how to move next. In their time together at Company G, Greenwood had seen Danny handle his Colts but only on a training range. The ex-Ranger knew just how little drawing a gun and popping holes in a target, which did not shoot back, meant. One could not judge a man's true potential until seeing him in a shooting scrape; and Greenwood always tried to avoid taking chances as a Ranger. However, he knew some of Danny's exploits* and more than a little about the other's brother's prowess with a brace of Army Colts. Danny learned gun-handling from the same source that trained Dusty Fog, the man claimed to be the fastest gun in Texas. Maybe Danny lived up to the family tradition, for his father, Sheriff Hondo Fog, had a name for being a good man with a gun. During his work against the Caspar County cow thieves, Danny

* One is told in THE BAD BUNCH.

met, faced and beat Ed Wren, a fast hired killer, in a fair fight. That implied a speed which put Danny into a class beyond Greenwood's range.

Of course Greenwood could always take up the matter with bare hands, but he knew all too well Danny's potential as a rough-house fighter and wanted no part of the tall blond in that line. Although conscious of Stella's mocking, expectant gaze, Greenwood made no attempt to take reprisals for the blow.

At last Stella spoke. "It seems he doesn't want to make anything of it."

"Looks that way, ma'am," Danny agreed.

Stella gave a slight, pregnant pause, eyes on Greenwood, daring him to accept Danny's challenge. A slight frown creased her brow when the man still made no move; and her voice became chilling and contemptuous as she said: "Go fetch me my horse, Greenwood."

Normally, as Greenwood well knew, she would have sent the livery barn's owner to fetch her mount. Scowling at Danny, the ex-Ranger turned and slouched from the building. Danny knew he had made a dangerous enemy. Never would Greenwood forget the humiliation heaped upon him. Given a suitable opportunity, he would strike back at Danny. Being aware of that, Danny meant to give the other as little chance of revenge as constant alertness allowed.

"I'm sorry about the *sabino*, ma'am," Danny said after Greenwood left.

"I understand. Are you in Moondog on business?"

"Should I be?"

"If you should, I don't know the reason," she answered. "We've a quiet, peaceful and friendly little town here. Is that right, Mr. Bescaby?"

Emotions played momentarily on Bescaby's face as he looked from Danny to the woman and gunman. For an instant a faint glimmer of hope showed on the man's face, then it died as he found Stella's cold eyes and Wigg's mocking smile before him. ·

"Th—That's right, Miss Howkins," Bescaby said, his voice bearing the bitter undertones of despair.

"So I fail to see why we should attract the attentions of the Rangers when there are so many more places in greater need of your services," Stella went on, ignoring Bescaby after the question.

"How many Rangers have been here?" Danny asked, watching Stella's face.

If he hoped to shock some emotion out of the woman, he failed. Not by a flicker of an eyelid did she show that the words meant anything to her. Nor did Wigg give any sign that he might know of other Rangers in the area.

"You're the first that I've seen," Stella stated. "How about you, Mr. Bescaby. Have you seen any?"

"No, Miss Howkins."

Watching Bescaby closely as he had studied the woman, Danny could see no sign of held-back knowledge and doubted if a man as scared as Bescaby would be able to conceal his emotions.

"Did you expect to find any of your friends here?" Stella asked.

"Can't say I did," Danny replied, telling the truth as far as it went. Naturally he could not mention the fact that two more of his company worked undercover in the area.

"Will you be staying here long?" she went on.

Danny thought fast. Until Greenwood identified him —and gained a crack on the jaw for his treachery— Danny aimed to stay in town and pose as a drifting cowhand resting before finding a new riding chore. With the line closed to him, he needed to find a fresh reason for his presence.

"I'll be here for a spell, ma'am," he said meeting her careful scrutiny with an attitude of one telling the un-varnished truth. "There's been a bunch of owlhoots hitting the banks of small towns like this pretty regular and Captain Murat got word that they're headed this way. So he sent me down here to be on hand should they come."

Even if Stella contacted headquarters, Danny knew he could rely on the man at the other end to back up his story, or cover for him if she worded her question in a manner which did not explain his excuse.

On the face of it, Stella accepted his story, for she acted just right.

"As the bank's biggest depositor," she said with a smile, "I'm pleased to know that we have a Ranger on hand to guard our property. It's no secret that our local law leaves a lot to be desired. Still, we're a poor county and can't run to hiring men of Dallas Stoudemire's class—nor do we have any need to normally. My men don't cause trouble in town. Do they, Mr. Bescaby?"

"No!" The word popped like the cork from a bottle.

"Moondog prides itself on Mr. Bescaby," Stella told Danny. "He's the only quiet livery barn owner in the West."

"Sure is a change from most," Danny agreed. "I'll tend to my horse."

"Of course. I don't have a house in town and my place is too far out for you to make it your base, although you'll always be welcome to come visiting. But if you mention my name at the hotel I'm sure they will find you a room."

"Why, thank you kindly, ma'am. I'll do that."

"And I'll exp——hope that you keep me informed, let me know of any developments."

"Sure, ma'am. Say, I hear that you own most of the range in these parts."

"I do."

"Then you might warn your hands that I'll be doing considerable riding. Captain Murat wants me to try to stop them out of town if I can, and I don't want cowhands chasing after me, thinking I'm a cow thief."

"Feel free to go anywhere you wish," she answered calmly. "I'll warn my men."

Just as the woman turned to go. Danny decided to try something. "This bunch I'm after. They always send a couple of fellers into town to scout it, sometimes get them in as much as three weeks ahead of time. You haven't seen any strangers around in the past few weeks, have you?"

"I haven't," Stella stated. "How about you, Mr. Bescaby?"

"No, Miss Howkins, I've seen nobody."

If everything had been all right, Stella and Bescaby would have mentioned the two Rangers. Folks with money in a threatened bank usually showed real good memories when questioned about suspicious visitors. While the Rangers would not have made themselves conspicuous, Danny knew folks in a small town like Moondog must have seen them around and of all people the livery barn's owner ought to remember them.

"You could be on a bum steer, Ranger," Wigg remarked.

"Could be, but until Captain Murat calls me in, I'm staying here."

"We'll try to make your stay a happy one," Stella promised. "I'm sure everybody in town would want that. Wouldn't they, Mr. Bescaby?"

"Yes, Miss Howkins," Bescaby agreed.

Smiling, Stella turned and walked from the barn. Wigg gave Bescaby a long, cold warning stare and then swung about to follow his employer.

"Use that empty stall there, Ranger," Bescaby said, speaking in a louder voice than necessary. "I'll fetch hay and grain for your horse."

Danny led the *sabino* into the indicated stall and started to remove the saddle. He wondered how much of his story Stella believed. There was a mighty shrewd woman and nobody's fool. She seemed to have everybody in town buffaloed, or thought she had; her whole attitude showed that.

Usually a man in Bescaby's position would have been on hand to talk with his visitor, swapping news and gossip. On his return with a filled hay-net and a bucket of grain, Bescaby showed every sign of wanting to leave Danny's presence as soon as he could.

"You sure you haven't seen any strangers around town?" Danny asked. "One tall and red-headed, the other shorter, stocky."

Throwing a nervous look towards the front doors,

Bescaby shook his head. "No. There's been nobody like that around here."

Every instinct told Danny that the man lied, but he did not press the matter further. He would get nothing from a man as badly scared as Bescaby and might even have cause to regret any effort to force the issue.

Ignoring the owner's departure, Danny cared for his horse and saw it settled in. Then he went to the corral at the rear of the building and studied the animals in its confines. Neither of his friends' horses stood among the half-dozen in the corral and Danny began to feel worried. Of course the two Rangers might be scouting the surrounding country, or working on some ranch —no, not the latter; the only ranch in the area belonged to Stella Howkins, who hired a man familiar with all the personnel of Company G. Danny decided that he had better start his search for the other two as soon as possible. One glance at the sky told him that the day had advanced too far for him to make a start before dark. Returning to the barn, he gripped his saddle by the horn and swung it on to his shoulder. A glance at the side door showed Danny that Bescaby watched him through its slightly open crack, but he made no attempt to resume the conversation. Plenty of time for that after he won the town's confidence—and he knew the best method of doing so.

On leaving the barn, Danny stood for a moment and looked along Main Street. He saw no sign of Stella or her men and did not expect any trouble until it became obvious that he came to Moondog in search of the first pair of Rangers. In his examination of the street, Danny noted that telegraph wires ran from the Wells Fargo office opposite the saloon. A comforting sight. At least he could make rapid contact with the outside world should it become necessary. Even if the operator happened, as Danny did not doubt, to be in Stella's employ as well as drawing pay from the great freight outfit, the Ranger knew enough about handling a transmitting key to be able to get his message out of Moondog.

During his walk from the livery barn to the hotel,

Danny began to realize just how strong a hold Stella Howkins had on the town. A woman approaching along the sidewalk, after leaving one of the buildings, stared hard at Danny then hurriedly crossed the street. Sweeping the boards before his place, the storekeeper gave a startled glance and shot into his premises, closing the door behind him. A pair of loafers seated in front of the saloon suddenly rose and almost scuttled around the corner of the building out of sight. Danny looked into the saloon in passing and saw Wigg leaning against the bar.

It all became very clear to Danny. During the time he cared for his horse, word must have gone out as to his position in life. Nobody wanted to be questioned by him and made it plain they did not intend to give him the opportunity.

"If I'd got any sense at all," Danny mused, "I'd get on my horse and hightail it out of here and not come back until I'd at least three of the boys backing me." He glanced at the open door of the hotel and went on, "Trouble is, I never have good sense."

Having delivered that sentiment to himself, Danny entered the building. The first thing to meet his eyes was the sight of one of Howkins' hard-case bodyguards leaning with a proprietary air on the reception desk. Next, Danny turned his eyes to the girl behind the desk. She stood maybe five-foot-six in height and a black dress strove to hide a rich, mature figure beneath its severe lines. Brown hair taken tightly back in a bun did little to help a rather plain face, yet the girl might have looked better in different conditions; say when wearing a smile instead of that tight-lipped serious expression.

Walking to the desk and ignoring the hard-cases, Danny lowered his saddle to the floor. He removed his hat and smiled at the girl. "Howdy, ma'am. I'd like a room if you have one, please."

"This here is the Ranger Miss Howkins sent word about, Connie," the hard-case put in.

Danny swung to face the man, his smile gone and his face unfriendly. "I put my hand into the teeth of the last man who announced that I'm a Ranger," he warned.

"So?" growled the man.

"So if you're not out of here by the time I count five, I'll ram you feet-first and neck-deep into the wall and use your ears for a hat-rack. One—two——."

Suddenly the hard-case realized that Danny meant, if not to carry out his threat, to take violent exception to being identified as a Ranger. And from what he had already seen, the hard-case figured Danny could do it. A man did not find admittance to the Rangers unless he knew how to take care of himself in any company.

"No offence, Ranger!" he yelped. "Only Miss Howkins told me to see you got settled in."

"You've done it. Now let's miss you," Danny answered. "And when you see her, tell Miss Howkins that I'm all grown up. Why, I even go out back all alone, 'cepting on dark nights."

"What's that mean?" asked the hard-case, a man hired for brawn rather than sparkling brilliance.

"That I don't need wet-nursing, or folks holding my hand. I've been out on my own before now."

"I'll tell her, but she won't like it."

"Then she can complain to me, or write real formal to Captain Murat," Danny replied, conscious of the girl's eyes on him. "And I got to two in my count."

Without another word, the hard-case turned and headed for the door. Halting just before he left, the man threw a savage frown in the girl's direction. Then he swung on his heel and left the building.

"Miss Howkins won't like your disrespect," the girl warned.

"Maybe her taxes help pay my salary, ma'am," Danny answered with a grin, "but that don't mean she owns me."

The girl's brown eyes studied him for a long moment. Never had he seen such beautiful eyes; they had warmth, tenderness, yet seemed sorrowful and pleading. He felt uncomfortable at having to act the part of a swaggering rough before the girl, yet he knew it must be done. Only by showing the people of the town that Stella Howkins and her men need not be feared could he break the woman's grip on them.

"Can I do anything for you?" asked the girl.

"Like I said, ma'am. I'd like a room."

Opening the register which lay before her, the girl reached for a pen and said, "Name, please."

"Fog, Daniel James Fog, known as Danny to my friends. And yours?"

A slight touch of colour came to the girl's cheeks. "Is it important?"

"A man has to know who to call for if he needs a clean towel or something."

"You call for Pedro."

"*Your* name is Pedro?"

Just the slightest hint of a smile came to the girl's lips and transformed her face. Given a different hair-style, a more attractive dress and that smile, the plain girl disappeared and a right pretty young woman would take her place. Only the smile did not stay for long.

"Pedro's our bell-hop. He brings towels—or 'somethings' to the rooms.

"Shucks. I always like to deal with the top folks."

Dropping her eyes to the desk top, and blushing a little, the girl spoke hurriedly. "My name is Connie Hooper. Room twelve, Mr. Fog. It faces the rear.

"The name's Danny, and I'd rather have one overlooking the Main Street."

"I'm afraid they're all booked."

Which was most likely a lie, Danny decided. He doubted if the hotel ever had occupants in more than half of its rooms, drawing most of its trade from stagecoach passengers staying over for the night.

"Miss Howkins book them just now?" he asked.

"I can hardly——"

Before Connie finished, Danny reached out, took the register and swung it around. Connie grabbed the book, slamming it shut and jerking it off the counter.

Only before she did so, Danny had seen two things;

first, a page had been torn out of the book; second, the handwriting on the sheet before the missing page was small, neat—and familiar. The person who filled in details of visitors to the hotel and the writer of the request for Ranger assistance were one and the same.

## CHAPTER THREE

## The Ranger Made A Mistake

"It's against the rules for a guest to examine the register, Mr. Fog!" Connie snapped, banging the bell on the desk top.

"How about a lawman looking for information?" Danny answered.

"What kind of information?"

"I came here because there's a chance your bank might be robbed——"

Surprise and disappointment warred on the girl's face. "But I thought——"

Her voice came to an abrupt halt as she looked towards the side door along the passage. It opened and a man came out. When Connie mentioned Pedro being the bell-hop, Danny pictured a Mexican boy, or at best one in his teens. The man who left the room and slouched along the passage in answer to the bell's summons stood around six foot in height, with heavy shoulders and unshaven, mean face, and wore range clothes of Mexican style, a knife sheathed at his left side and Colt holstered on the right.

"You wan' something, *senorita*?" he growled.

"Are you Pedro?" Danny put in before the girl could reply.

"Tha's me."

"Tote my saddle up to room twelve. Nope, make it one of the front rooms."

"But I thought——," the Mexican began.

"Thinking's plumb bad for a man," Danny interrupted. "Choya Santoval started thinking, friend, and look where it got him."

A scowl creased Pedro's surly face as he looked at Danny. There had been a time when Choya Santoval seemed set to revive the good old days of *Comanchero* raids in Texas. Only he and his band made the mistake of ambushing a party of Rangers—and not finishing them all off. Danny, sole survivor of the Ranger trio, took up the trail and with the aid of Calamity Jane, wrote *finis* to Santoval's band.

"I don't know Santoval," Pedro growled in a voice that showed he lied.

"Shouldn't think a *bell-hop* would. I'll take the front room at the end, if it's empty, ma'am. Don't figure Miss Howkins'd mind, her being the bank's biggest depositor and all. I can't cover the street and the bank from a room at the rear."

"Well, I——," Connie began.

"Tell you what I'll do," Danny went on. "I'll take full responsibility."

"*Senorita Howkins* said——," Pedro began.

"Santoval talked too much, *hombre*," Danny growled. "It's near on as bad as thinking, they do tell me. Tote my gear upstairs and put it in the room I told you."

For a moment Pedro hesitated. Then he decided not to take up the Ranger's obvious challenge. While having orders from his employer to keep an eye on Danny, he had not been given instructions as to how the Ranger must be treated. So he decided to use his judgement and his appraisal of the situation which warned him not to push the blond Texan too far.

"Put Mr. Fog where he *demands*," Connie ordered, laying great stress on the last word and clearly paving the way for herself to explain the disobedience should she be taken to task over allowing Danny the use of a room overlooking the main street. When Stella Howkins protested, Connie could claim that Danny forced the room from her and that Pedro failed to stop him.

With a face almost black in anger, Pedro picked up Danny's saddle and carried it towards the stairs. When the Mexican had gone from sight, Danny turned to the girl and smiled.

"What did you think brought me here, ma'am?" he asked.

"I—Oh, nothing. What were you saying about the bank being robbed?"

"Only that we thought it might be," he explained and went on with the same story he told to Stella Howkins. "See, ma'am, the way the gang works that they always send in a couple of scouts and get the lie of the land. I was wondering if you'd seen them, or if they'd been rooming here. That's why I wanted to look at the register."

"Do they always use the same names?"

"Near enough the same. Always something like Baxter and Dennison. They were Braxted and Deneson in Caspar City, Dexter and Benson in Sherwood. Aren't what you might call real smart outlaws."

For a long moment the girl studied his face, however, she made no attempt to take out the register.

"I'm sorry," she said. "You see, I spilled ink all over the page with the recent roomers on it and had to tear it out of the book."

"And you can't remember those two fellers? One about my height, slimmer and with red hair; the other shorter, stocky and sporting a moustache like a set of bull's horns."

"I'm afraid I can't help you," the girl answered, throwing a glance at the stairs. "Can you, Pedro?"

Turning, Danny saw the Mexican standing on the stairs. Pedro came down to the ground floor and approached the desk.

"I forgot the key to the room, *senorita*," he said. "What you want to know about, Ranger?"

"Figured you'd heard," Danny grunted. "Did you

see the two fellers I was asking about?''

"They was never in Moondog," Pedro answered.
"Maybe the Ranger made a mistake and they go
another town."

"Maybe I did," Danny agreed. "Only until I hear
different from Captain Murat I'm staying right here.
Reckon I'll go to my room now, ma'am. You can give
me the key and I'll tote my gear in myself."

Putting on his hat, Danny nodded to the girl and
walked by Pedro to the foot of the stairs. Without
another look at the Mexican, Danny started to go up to
the first floor. As he expected, his saddle lay at
the top of the stairs. Taking up the saddle, he glanced
back and saw Pedro standing watching him. Danny
walked around the corner into the passage and from
Pedro's sight. Laying down the saddle quietly, Danny
removed his hat and advanced cautiously to the head of
the stairs. He peered around the corner carefully and,
seeing no sign of Pedro, started down the stairs as silently as he could manage. Before he reached the halfway level, he heard voices from below.

"*Senorita* Howkins won't like him not going where
she said," Pedro announced.

"Then why didn't you stop him?" answered the girl.
"That's what you're here for, isn't it? To enforce Stella
Howkins' will upon people."

"I don't know what that means," growled the
Mexican. "If I thought——"

"You had better let Miss Howkins know what happened," Connie interrupted, ignoring the man's scowling face.

On the stairs Danny tensed ready to cut in should the
Mexican lay hands on the girl. However, Pedro con-
tented himself with spitting out a string of Mexican
curses directed at the girl and Danny, then turned and
stamped off along the passage into the room the bell's
summons brought him from. Danny relaxed and turned
to go silently back up the stairs. From what he had just
seen, one person in town did not seem afraid of the
Howkins outfit. There might be more, but Danny knew

he must take his time in finding them. He decided to leave further discussion with the girl until a more opportune moment.

The room Danny entered proved to be clean, neat and comfortable. In addition to a lock, the door offered a set of bolts as extra protection for the guests, and a stout chair stood by the wash-stand. With the bolts closed, the lock turned and the chair in place, Danny reckoned he could sleep safely. However, he took precautions. First he checked that the bed stood in a position which nobody outside could lay bead with a rifle. The window appeared to be well-secured but there was a balcony outside. Knowing himself to be a light sleeper, Danny decided he could not be approached from the window without the noise waking him.

While at the window, Danny looked down at Moondog's main street. From his position it looked no different from any other town. People moved about on the street or stood and talked. Yet he sensed something different, an undercurrent that he could not put his finger on. Then he got it. None of the people below him smiled or laughed. It even seemed that they were afraid to gather together for any length of time, for they would meet, exchange a few words, darting nervous glances around, and then go their separate ways.

Turning from the window, Danny removed his gunbelt and went to the bed. He sat down, took out his Colts and checked them over. Every instinct told him that he might need the guns before he left Moondog and in that case must be able to rely on their correct functioning if he wished to stay alive.

Night came and Danny left his room to begin the task of giving the citizens of Moondog confidence, so that they might stand up against Stella Howkins' men. After eating a lonely meal in the dining room, Danny left the hotel and strolled along the darkened streets towards the Blue Bull saloon. He had seen Connie hovering in the background while he ate, but Pedro also stood in a position where he could watch, so Danny did not attempt to talk with the girl.

Pushing open the doors of the saloon, Danny stepped inside and looked around him. Although a fair crowd of townsmen were present, they made little noise and gathered in small, quietly talking groups. Danny saw a trio of hard-cases, including Howkins' bodyguard, but the rancher's brother was not present. Behind the bar, a tall, slim, studious-looking young man with a pallid face dispensed the drinks. He did not look much like the usual type of man one saw behind the western bar.

What little noise there had been died off as Danny entered. He walked across the room and halted at the bar, close to one of the groups of townsmen.

"Beer, friend," he told the bartender. "And take something for yourself."

"Thanks, but I never drink while I'm working," smiled the bartender, his voice and tones that of a well-educated man.

"That's a real good rule to live by," Danny commented and looked at the nearest bunch of customers. "Any of you gents who aren't working care for something?"

Scared expressions came to several faces, eyes swivelling to where the Lazy H men sat watching every move.

"He don't look so much," the man who had not been at the livery barn stated.

"You go try him, Furst," grunted one of the other two.

Furst thrust back his chair, rose and swaggered across the room to halt between Danny and the townsmen. A grin creased his face and he jerked a thumb to the bartender.

"Pour me four fingers of Old Stump Blaster, Harvey," he ordered. "It's not every day I get chance to take a drink that a Ranger pays for. It's usually the other way round, they make you buy for them."

"Leave the bottle, friend," Danny cut in as the bartender turned to fulfill the order.

"Pour it, Harvey, I've never yet had a drink from a

Ranger!'' repeated the hard-case, throwing a grin in his friends' direction.

"I've got news for you, hombre," Danny drawled, his voice loud enough to carry around the room. "You still haven't had one."

"You said——"

"My offer didn't include two-bit gun-slicks."

Never had any man in Moondog defied Furst, for when he took on the Lazy H payroll the submission of the town had already become a fact. Swinging towards Danny, Furst stared at the Ranger in surprise. A glance in the bar's mirror showed Furst that every eye in the room took in the scene. Clearly he must establish his superiority over the blond Texan. So, with that thought in mind, Furst made what he fondly believed was the correct answer to Danny's words.

Furst's right hand rose, the elbow bending as he started to draw his Colt. Only Danny moved faster and in a manner the hard-case never expected. Maybe Danny could have taken Furst in a down-grab-and-shoot fracas, but he knew of a better way to impress the watching townsmen. Out stabbed Danny's left hand, palm upwards, to clamp hold of and push at the bend of Furst's right elbow. In the same move Danny caught and pulled the man's right shoulder with his other hand. Although Furst's Colt left the holster, he could not bring it into use. The instant Danny obtained the hold, he pivoted around until he stood alongside and slightly to the rear of Furst. As Danny did not release his grip, he brought the man's arm around and up in an outside bar hammerlock which was both effective and painful, forcing his back towards the roof. Keeping his upper arm and torso pressing against Furst, Danny held the hard-case. He saw Furst's companions start to rise and prepared to copper their bet. Releasing the shoulder, but still holding the elbow. Danny twisted the Colt from Furst's grasp. In a quick chopping motion, Danny brought the butt of the gun on to Furst's head. Even as the man collapsed, Danny whirled the Colt into a firing position and threw down on the other two men.

"Just hold it right there!" he ordered.

Once again Danny's words and actions brought an end to any hostile movements the two hard-cases might have made. Half-risen from their seats, hands still not on gun butts, they froze under the threat of a lined gun.

"You'd no cause to jump Furst that ways," stated one of the men indignantly.

"Go complain to the mayor about it," Danny replied. "Make a start at it right now. And take him," he jerked a contemptuous thumb towards the groaning man at his feet, "with you."

Slowly and sullenly the two hard-cases left their table and moved forward. They helped Furst to his feet, supporting him between them as they prepared to leave the building. Before the men could go, Danny's cold, mocking voice halted them.

"Hey! Take your pard's gun. He might run across a half-blind, one-armed midget he can scare."

With that Danny threw the gun under-hand to the nearest man. Making a wild grab, and almost losing his hold on Furst, the man caught the Colt by its chamber. The instant his fingers closed around the cold steel, the hard-case realized how much of an offensive advantage he now possessed. However, any joy he might have felt rapidly became tempered and weakened by what he saw. Danny stood with feet apart, legs slightly bent, right hand still in the throwing position and well clear of either of the staghorn-butted Colts—but his left hand twisted palm outwards a scant couple of inches from the turned-forward butt of the near-side weapon.

Knowing he would never take a chance like that unless full sure he could draw and shoot before the man who caught the gun could turn it his way, the hard-case doubted if Danny would think differently. So he called off any thoughts he held for avenging Furst and re-establishing Lazy H's social standing. Instead he decided to make an attempt at explaining away his failure to take action.

"Furst's head's bleeding bad," he said. "We'd best get him to the doctor."

"Be best," agreed his companion, knowing the injury did not need medical attention and also that the doctor sat at a table in the saloon. However, he decided to cover up their rout. While his pard thrust Furst's gun into his waistband, the second man eyed Danny and growled, "A feller could get hurt tossing guns about like you do."

"I know," Danny replied. "The last time I did it, the feller caught the gun and tried to turn it and shoot me—I'm still here."

Once again Danny threw down the gauntlet, but neither of the Lazy H men made any attempt to take it up. Although both of the hard-cases knew they were backing down and that the very men they were supposed to impress witnessed their failure. Danny's tough self-confidence made them afraid to try to change the situation. By now both knew Danny's name and that, as much as his being a member of the tough, efficient, gun-handy Texas Rangers, caused the hard-cases to think twice before offering to tangle with him. Supporting the groaning Furst between them, they left the saloon watched by every local man present.

Not so Danny. Playing his role to the end, he calmly swung back to the bar and rested his elbows upon its top. Although offering his back to the men, Danny took the precaution of keeping an eye on them through the bar mirror. Not until the trio had passed out of sight did he relax and turn to see how his actions had been received by his audience.

"How about that drink *now*, gents?" he asked, and without waiting for an answer turned to the bartender. "Set them up, friend. I'll take it kind that you gents bend an elbow with me."

His tone implied that he would also take grave exception at anybody refusing to accept his offer. With a smile, faint but there, the bartender started to reach for glasses. Danny thought that there might be a thawing

once he cleared the Lazy H men from the room. Having
looked around, he could see no sign of more of the
hard-cases present. Then he noticed the scared glances
the men at the bar threw in a certain direction.
Following the direction of the glances, he studied the
trio of men who sat at a table by the left wall.

Not one of the trio looked like a gun-fighting hard-
case. In fact all gave the impression of being town
dwellers, civic dignitaries almost. All wore good
clothing and the bottle on the table before them belonged to the saloon's best stock. The biggest member
of the trio thrust back his chair and rose. He wore a grey
suit, silk cravat with a diamond stick-pin, fancy vest,
and looked pompous, corpulent, with just a shade of ar-
rogance in his side-whiskered face.

"Come along, gentlemen," he boomed. "Is this the
hospitality of our fair city of Moondog? Accept our
visitor's offer. I'll have a glass of my usual, Harvey."

With that the man strode across the room. Second of
the trio, a sallow-faced thin man in sober black, glanced
at the third, a burly, rough-looking cuss, whose clothing
appeared much too good for him. Although both
looked puzzled by the big man's actions, they followed
him to the bar and ordered drinks.

"Sure hope Cap'n Jules'll let me take this lot off as
expenses," Danny thought as man after man accepted
his offer.

"My name is Tuttle, mayor of Moondog and
president of the bank," the big man boomed. "I'd like
you to meet my friends. This is Doctor Drager."

"Doc," Danny greeted the thin man, and seeing his
guess at Drager being the local undertaker was wrong.

"Sterling Kimble, he runs the general store and post
office," Tuttle went on, indicating the third of his
party. "John Weaver, our blacksmith."

Danny had guessed at Weaver's employment. The
burly blacksmith looked ready to burst the seams of his
own suit, and had heft enough not to be afraid of any
man. Yet he seemed almost scared in the presence of the
town's leading citizens.

"I'll fetch my *sabino* down for you to look over, if I can," Danny told Weaver, but the man did not show any great eagerness at receiving a prospective customer.

"You probably know Mr. Bescaby from the livery barn," Tuttle said. "Look, we're wasting drinking time with all these introductions. You boys can tell the Ranger your own names, I'm setting up another round of drinks."

While the setting-up took place, Danny examined Bescaby in better light than offered by the shady barn. The man's face struck Danny as interesting and significant. A faint scar showed over one eye; the left ear bore a characteristic thickening of tissue; and the nose had been broken. Maybe Bescaby received the facial damage at the hands of the Lazy H men, but Danny thought that the marks had been there for some years. A man with such a face ought not allow a skinny, puny runt like young Howkins to slap him around or abuse him.

"And what do you think of our town, Ranger?" boomed Tuttle, cutting in on Danny's thoughts.

"Nice lil place. Only one thing though."

"What's that?" growled Kimble, throwing a worried glance at Tuttle.

"Somebody in it's sure got a few strange notions."

"If you mean those three——," Tuttle began.

"Shucks, they weren't nothing but a bunch of mean-mouthed bullies and don't count for a thing," Danny answered. "I was thinking about the saloon sign, It's right smart, only——"

"You never saw a bull that colour," interrupted the bartender. "Everybody says it sooner or later."

"All right," Danny grinned. "I'll buy it."

"There's nothing to buy," the bartender replied. "Paint isn't the easiest thing to lay hands on in Moon-dog and blue was the only colour I could get in sufficient quantity to handle the bulk of the subject."

"Harvey's quite an artist, Ranger," Tuttle declared in his professional hand-shaker's voice. "A young man of considerable talent."

"I only wish the art critics in the East thought that," Harvey sighed.

Alert and watchful, Danny caught a sign flashed from Tuttle to Kimble. The postmaster scowled, received another more vigorous signal, and called in a round of drinks; an action which appeared to surprise the group at the bar.

Danny realized that the three men were trying to jolly things up, to make the atmosphere less strained and obviously wrong. It appeared that the young Ranger had not cleared all the Lazy H men from the room.

## CHAPTER FOUR

## If You Can't Prove You're A Ranger, I'll Kill You!

Apparently, having to buy a round of drinks did not please Kimble. He scowled at Danny and said, "Can't say I go for a lawman abusing law-abiding citizens."

A man did not need the powers of a Comanche witch woman to figure that the mayor, doctor and post master worked for Stella Howkins, so Danny accorded Kimble the same treatment as any other Lazy H hand.

"Can't say that I asked you about it," he replied.

Cold fury worked on Kimble's face, but prudence kept his anger in check. If Furst, Matic and Cheem could not handle the Ranger, Kimble doubted if he would have better luck.

"As justice of the peace hereabouts——," he began.

"Now, Sterling," Tuttle put in. "The Ranger handled things as he saw fit."

"It's not good for a lawman to act that way," Kimble growled sullenly.

"I always learned that fear was the basis of all respect," Danny drawled. "That jasper fixed to disrespect the Rangers and I stopped him. Which same I reckon folks'll respect the law more if they know they can't get away with pushing around or mean-mouthing the fellers handling it."

"A shrewd observation," boomed Tuttle. "Come on, Doc, when was the last time you called in a round of drinks?"

"Not for me just now," Danny said. "I just thought. I'm nearly late for calling in to Captain Murat."

37

"Huh?" grunted Tutle, face startled. "Is Murat near here?"

"Over to Carrintown," Danny answered, seeing Kimble and Drager exchange scared glances.

Relief came to Tuttle's face as he realized that the Ranger captain was over a day's hard ride away.

"How do you check in?" the banker asked.

"That's Ranger business."

"Well, you *are* here to guard my bank. I feel that I'm entitled to know a little of your plans."

"Why sure," Danny agreed. "But they're secret orders. Hell, I know that all these gents here are honest, but talk might get out."

"We could go to my office," Tuttle suggested.

"Shucks, that table across there'll do if we hold down our voices," Danny answered, then shook his head as Drager and Kimble turned with Tuttle. "That's for Mr. Tuttle and nobody else."

Once more fury mottled Kimble's face. "Damn it to hell! I'm just——"

The words died away as Danny, who had begun to turn from the bar, swung back again and clearly showed that, as far as he was concerned, the matter had come to an end.

Throwing a warning scowl at Kimble, the banker intervened. "The Ranger's only following his orders, Sterling. You stay here. Come with me, Ranger."

While walking across the room with Kimble, Danny thought fast. He knew he had put himself in a very dangerous position and sought for a means of easing the situation, relieving the danger to his life. Stella Howkins ruled Moondog by fear and through the toughness of her men. Already Danny had cut in and defied her power at least three times. If she hoped to keep her hold over the people of the town, she must teach him a sharp lesson; kill him even. So Danny wanted something to keep her from giving the order which would send men after his hide. Not that Danny was in a panic. He had sense enough to realize his danger, and he did not wish to die. While he reckoned he could take care of himself in an open fight, Danny knew he could not watch his back or guard against ambush twenty-four hours a day. He must figure out some way to make the Lazy H hold its hand.

Remembering the concern shown by Tuttle's party when he mentioned notifying Captain Murat, Danny thought up a scheme that might work. He elaborated on it as he walked and on halting in the center of the room put it into operation.

"It's like this," he told Tuttle in a low, confidential voice. "We're not sure just which town that gang'll hit next. So Captain Murat's got a man staked down in several small places. Now that gang always hits in the evening, between sundown and eight or so at night. So he's waiting in Carrintown and each of us has to send word to him. It he doesn't get the word he starts out right away with the rest of the company, headed for the feller who doesn't send it."

"I see," Tuttle breathed. "And what might the word be?"

"It's changed every night," Danny replied, still thinking fast and planning his moves. "Sent to the sheriff's office in Carrintown. Only one word so's to save time and keep the wires clear."

"Shouldn't you tell me the word so I can——"

"Shucks, the only way I won't be able to send off word each night'll be because the gang've hit. When that happens, the sooner Captain Jules starts riding, the better."

"Of course," Tuttle agreed, but his voice had lost all its pompous boom. "A commendable scheme. I don't see our telegraphist here, so he must still be in his office. If you wish, I'll come with you."

"Shucks, mayor, you stop on here with your friends," Danny replied. "I reckon I can cross the street to the Wells Fargo office without help."

Despite Danny's assurance, Tuttle followed him from the saloon. The banker halted on the sidewalk, slapping his hands on his waistband and sucked in a deep breath.

"Love the smell of sage," he said, not following

Danny on to the street. "I reckon I'll just take a breath of air before I——Look out, Ranger, to your left!"

The last words came in a yell. Instantly Danny whirled around, dropping to the wheel-rutted dirt of the street. Flame lanced from the alley at the left of the saloon, the muzzle-blast of a roaring gun momentarily showing a shape standing just at the edge of the building. Had Danny moved just a shade slower, or kept his feet, he would have been hit. Even as he fell, he felt the wind of a close-passing bullet on his ear. A startled curse rose from the man who was shot, dying half-completed. Even as Danny landed on the ground, he fanned off three shots in reply to the other man's lead. On the last shot, Danny rolled over three times, landing on his stomach with the Colt ready to fire again. However, while rolling he had seen the dark shape at the edge of the building jerk, stagger and fall.

Cautiously Danny came to his feet. With his gun held ready for use, he walked forward, making for the shape lying in the alley. Feet thudded in the saloon and men ran towards the doors, bursting out on to the sidewalk. Questions were shouted but received no answers, then the customers from the saloon followed Tuttle along the sidewalk to where Danny stood looking down into the alley.

"Who is it, Ranger?" Tuttle asked.

"Come and strike a match and look," Danny replied.

Tuttle obeyed Danny's request and the crowd moved forward. However, Danny kept back out of the brief light of a struck match. He guessed at the identity of his attacker and knew that other guns might be waiting for a chance to sight on him. There was no point in taking chances until after word of his position filtered to the Lazy H.

Standing in the forefront of the crowd, Kimble looked down at the man who tried, and failed, to kill the Ranger. Then Kimble's eyes lifted to Tuttle's face and suspicion edged his voice as he said: "It's Furst! What the hell, Tuttle?"

Most people would have taken the words to be a

query about Furst's reason for being found dead. Danny knew that Kimble demanded an explanation from Tuttle why the banker gave a warning that saved the Ranger's life.

"He must have been after the Ranger and looking for even," Tuttle replied.

"Yes," Drager put in, sounding puzzled, "but why——"

"Because of the way the Ranger handled him inside!" Tuttle almost yelled. "You'd better go send your message, Ranger."

"How about him?" Danny said.

"We'll attend to him for you. Nobody blames you for acting as you did. I'm only grateful that I happened to see him and warn you in time."

"Feel a mite that way about it myself," Danny admitted.

"Then you'd better leave me handle things here. I don't think Captain Murat would be very pleased if he brought his men here for no good reason."

"You could be right at that, Mr. Tuttle," Danny said. "I'll go to the telegraph office right now."

"Take Furst to the undertaker's parlour, some of you," Tuttle ordered as Danny walked across the street.

Four men laid hold of the body and lifted it. Most of the others walked away and only a few of them entered the saloon. Just as Tuttle turned to go back into the bar, Kimble caught his arm and held him.

"All right, Tut——!"

"Not here, you fool!" Tuttle snarled, throwing the hand from his sleeve. "He might be watching us from the Wells Fargo office. Let's go down the alley. If he asks, we'll say we went to see if Matic and Cheem were about."

All three men went into the alley and along half of its length before they halted. In a voice raw and dripping with suspicion, Kimble demanded to be told why Tuttle acted in such a manner.

"I can explain," Tuttle replied.

"It'd better be good, *hombre*!" growled a voice.

The bulky shapes of Matic and Cheem loomed out of the darkness, and each hard-case held a gun. Cheem, the man who Danny evicted from the hotel, moved close to Tuttle, his voice charged with menace:

"Furst could have cut that damned Ranger down——"

"And by nightfall tomorrow, at the latest, Captain Murat'd be here with a company of Rangers at his back," Tuttle answered, going on to tell the story Danny passed on to him.

"It's lucky you yelled then," Drager breathed. "We can hold this town down while there's only one, or two, Rangers in here——"

Swinging towards the thin man, Tuttle thrust a furious face up close and spat angry words into the other's startled features.

"There's only been one Ranger here. Don't you ever forget it for a minute."

"What if he learns about the other two?" Matic asked.

"Nobody'd risk telling him while he's alone," Tuttle replied. "Anyway, all he could learn was that a couple of men came to town, stayed a few days and pulled out one night."

"Sure. We didn't learn they was Rangers until——," Kimble put in.

"But he's come looking for them!" Drager interrupted.

"That's possible," Tuttle admitted. "Although I can't see Murat sending a lone man in when two of his company had gone missing. Fog could be here for the reason he told me, because of a threatened bank raid. Anyway, you pair had best make a fast run to the Lazy H and tell Miss Howkins how it happened."

"And make damned sure she understands about the messages Fog has to send out every night," Drager said, his face working nervously. "We can't let anything happen to him now."

At the Wells Fargo office Danny wrote his message on an official company form and passed it to the fat man behind the desk. After reading the message, the agent jerked his face to Danny's, piggy eyes glinting worriedly under the green eye-shade.

"The mayor said for me to tell you it's all right," Danny said. "Go ask him if you like. Or I'll send it myself."

"Y—You know how to handle a telegraph key?"

"Sure. Always figured it would come in handy some day."

Sinking into his chair, the agent reached for the knob of his telegraph key. He rattled off the message, not daring to make a slip, for the blond Texan's grey eyes watched him all the time.

Danny waited until his message went over the wires, then left the office. For a time his life would be safe. The sheriff at Carrintown had long been an active supporter of the Rangers and could be relied upon not to send a message asking about the few lines dispatched under Danny's name.

Once Danny glanced through the office window and saw five shapes emerge from the left side alley of the saloon. Recognizing all five, he grinned to himself. Soon, if the way the two hard-cases mounted their horses was anything to go on, Stella Howkins would hear this story. He did not doubt that she would want him kept alive until she checked on the truth of it. That ought to take her a few days and with any amount of luck Captain Murat should have some help on hand, or very close, by then.

Visiting the saloon, Danny found that most of the customers had taken advantage of the shooting to slip off to their homes. Doubtless they wanted to disassociate themselves from any part of his company. He did not care, for he knew that he had made a real good start at building up their courage.

After taking another beer with Tuttle, and assuring the mayor that he sent off his message, Danny walked from the saloon and back to the hotel. Although the hall was empty, Danny noticed that Pedro's door stood open. Crossing the hall quickly, Danny hurried upstairs and to his room. He let himself in and closed the door. On turning up the lamp, he looked around. Nothing had been disturbed, his bedroll lay where he left it, the war bag still unopened.

Just as Danny took off his gunbelt, a knock sounded on the door. Drawing his right-hand Colt, he asked who was outside.

"It's me, Pedro, *senor*."

"What do you want?"

"I have brought you water and towels. I forget them earlier and the *senorita* told me to fetch them as soon as you came in."

Opening the door, Danny allowed Pedro to enter. He saw that the Mexican told the truth about visiting, for Pedro carried a large water-filled jug in one hand and a couple of towels in the other. Darting glances around the room, Pedro crossed to the washstand and set down his burden.

"You sure take good care of your roomers," Danny remarked sardonically, as the Mexican went to the window and tried to raise it.

"The *senorita* wants it that way," grunted Pedro. "You want for me to open the window?"

"Nope. Figure I'll get all the fresh air I want if I have to take out after those owlhoots."

"Have you everything you want, *senor*?" Pedro went on, going to the bed and peering under it.

"You can tell me that, I've not looked," Danny replied. "Is it there?"

"No—*Si, senor*, it's there. Only sometimes the woman who does the rooms forgets to fetch it back."

"Then maybe I can get some sleep?"

"*Si, senor*. But——"

"I know, the *senorita* likes everything comfortable for her guests. Why not look in the wardrobe, see there's no mice to disturb me?"

Turning, Pedro threw a suspicious glance at the small wardrobe and took a step towards it. Then he let out an annoyed grunt and swung to face Danny. For a moment Pedro glared at the smiling Texan, then stamped out of the room. Walking to the door, Danny shot the bolts and turned the key in the lock.

An admiring smile twisted his lips as he returned to his bed and undressed. Stella Howkins appeared to have thought out most angles. Not for a moment did Danny think that Pedro's visit had anything to do with concern for a guest's comfort. The Mexican came to check that Danny had not brought somebody from the town with him for a talk in the privacy of the room.

Climbing into bed, Danny put his gunbelt where he could reach the Colts with the minimum of fumbling. Then he turned down the lamp and made himself comfortable. The long hard ride to reach Moondog and his activities since arriving were inducements to sleep, and Danny soon drifted off.

Danny woke, stirring slightly in his bed and right hand reaching to draw its waiting Colt. For a few seconds he lay without moving, ears strained to catch some idea of what jolted him from sleep. Slowly his eyes went around the room, picking the shapes of the various furnishings and halting at the lighter square of the window. Even as he watched, a hand appeared at the outside and fingers tapped gently upon the glass.

Gun in hand, and clad only in his long-legged underpants, Danny slipped silently from the bed, landing on the floor. He stayed down low as he wriggled to the wall alongside the window. Again the fingers drummed on the glass, this time with a more impatient sound. Reaching the wall, Danny rose and flattened himself out. He kept himself clear of the window frame and held his Colt ready for use.

Reaching out a hand, he unfastened the window's catch and inched up the sash until a small gap showed at the bottom.

"Who is it?" he breathed.

"Let me in," whispered a feminine voice.

"Come round and show yourself first."

The order received prompt obedience as a dark shape moved in front of the window. A hooded cloak hid the identity of Danny's caller, but he guessed it to be the

woman who spoke. Anyhow, he doubted if Stella
Howkins would be planning anything against him so
soon after he put out his bluff.

"Let me in quickly," the hooded shape demanded,
voice just a shade high with tension.

"Sure, ma'am," he replied. "Only I reckon you
ought to know I've got a gun in my hand and that I'll
cut loose on anybody but you who comes in."

After delivering his warning, Danny eased the sash
higher and moved back. Alert for trouble, he watched
the shape climb awkwardly through the window. For
once in his life Danny laid aside chivalry and polite
behaviour, letting the girl climb into the room unaided.

"Don't light the lamp yet!" she warned.

Suddenly aware of his state of undress, Danny could
not hold down a grin at the words. "Ma'am," he said,
"that's the last thing I aimed to do."

Turning, Danny's visitor—he still could not be sure
of her identity—drew the window drapes. In the brief
moment before the light from the window was gone
Danny noticed that the girl only used one hand, keeping
the other beneath her cloak.

"You can light the lamp now," she said when the
drapes closed.

"Not just yet, ma'am," Danny answered, feeling his
way to the bed.

"I don't see why——"

"And I sure hope you never do," Danny interrupted,
putting down his Colt and reaching for his levis.

Danny pulled on his pants and shirt, then struck a
match and crossed the room to light the lamp. Not until
it glowed did he turn his attention to his visitor but when
he did, he received something of a surprise.

In entering the room her hood had slipped back. She
looked a piece more attractive with her hair down instead of held in that tight bun, especially as she wore a
flannel nightgown under the cloak and it showed she
possessed a shapely figure. Kiowa moccasins covered
her feet and dainty ankles peeped from under the hem
of the nightgown. A pretty picture to wake a man in the

early hours of the morning, if one overlooked the shotgun she held, its barrels lined straight on Danny's favourite belly.

With his Colt lying just too far away for a swift grab, Danny did the wisest thing under the circumstances, nothing. He looked down at the gun, one of the twenty-inch, twin barrel, ten gauge models produced for Wells Fargo; a short, handy weapon and deadly in skilled hands. If the way the girl held it proved anything she was handy enough to hit her mark. Even if she had never held a gun before in her life, at that range she could not miss him.

"I don't know what you have in mind, ma'am——," he began.

"It's simple," she replied. "If you can't prove you're a Ranger, I'll kill you."

# CHAPTER FIVE

## You're In A Town Of Cowards, Mr. Fog

For a time Danny looked at the yawning muzzle of the ten-gauge, then he grinned and asked, "Reckon you wouldn't just take my word, ma'am?"

Despite the tension which lined her face, the girl managed a weak smile in return. "You reckon right, I wouldn't."

"How about if I show you my badge?"

"Greenwood has one," Connie Hooper pointed out, "but he's no Ranger."

Interest flickered on Danny's face. "The hell you s——sorry, ma'am. Only I saw Captain Murat take Greenwood's badge from him when we booted him out of our Company, and he didn't have two."

"He still has one. I saw him showing it to Pedro," the girl replied and for a moment the shotgun's barrels sagged a trifle.

"When was this?" Danny asked.

"About a week ago. But you still haven't proved to me that you are a Ranger."

"How about this?" asked Danny. "I realize that Moondog is only a small town with little pull politically, but I would point out that we pay our share of the State's taxes and should be in a small way able to expect that the Texas Rangers afford us the same protection as they give to other, larger, better policed areas."

The shotgun's muzzle sank to the floor and did not rise. Connie nodded gravely and said, "That was in the second letter I sent to Captain Murat."

"Which was posted in Carrintown," Danny replied. "I read the letter, as the Captain's away on furlough."

"And you came alone?"

"I was the only Ranger on the post who was fit to travel. But there was no time to waste. It looked like the first two men sent had disappeared."

"Two——The two men you asked about?"

"Sure. Put down the scatter and take a seat while we talk this out."

"You must think I'm terrible, writing the way I did in the second letter," she said, laying the shotgun on the bed and taking a seat primly on the room's only chair.

"Nope. I figured you needed help bad. Say, how did you get here?"

"Through the next room and along the balcony."

"How about Miss Howkins' watchdog?" Danny asked.

"I accidentally left a full bottle of whisky on the desk. Pedro won't be around for a spell."

"And why'd you come here?" Danny went on.

"To find out if you really were a Ranger," she answered.

"And kill me if I wasn't?"

She nodded soberly. "Yes. Then I would have claimed that you asked me to bring something to your room. Only I felt suspicious and brought my shotgun. When you attacked me, I had to shoot."

Studying the girl's face, Danny found himself believing every word she said. "Why'd you want to do that?"

"Because if you weren't a Ranger, then you pretended to be one, so Stella Howkins could learn who might have courage enough to stand against her when the real Rangers came."

"And if she found out?" asked Danny.

"A man tried to send for the sheriff once. He made the mistake of mailing the letter here in town. That night the feed barn he owned went up in flames. Stella Howkins doesn't intend to have anybody breaking her grip on the town."

"And how about when the sheriff comes for tax collecting or something?"

"A few of her men are in town all the time, and as justice of the peace Kimble is at the sheriff's side all the time."

"It was the same down the saloon tonight," Danny said. "The mayor and his two *amigos* were with the crowd, and three of her men. They've got this town sewed up good. What I want to know is why they want it that way."

"For money, of course," Connie stated. "Through the bank she has control of every business in town. I don't know about the rest, but when I've made my interest repayments, I've barely enough left over to live on."

"Sure, but what she makes out of the town would barely cover the hire of her hands. I reckon she runs a fair-sized crew."

"Thirty or forty hired guns," the girl answered.

"And they don't come at thirty-a-month-and-found," Danny pointed out. A feller like Wigg pulls in a hundred and twenty-five dollars a month at least. Mind, I doubt if she's many as good as Wigg."

"Pedro gets seventy-five," Connie said bitterly. "I know because I have to pay it."

"That's just one man," Danny told her. "Nope, Connie gal, there's more to this than just holding down a tw—one-horse town for what she'd make from it. There just has to be. Tell me all you can."

"She bought the old Rocking V about eighteen months ago. It covered quite a fair piece of land. Made a book purchase of it."

"That's not unusual," Danny commented. "Hold it though. That'd be about the time the big blue norther hit, wouldn't it?"

"Yes," agreed Connie.

"We missed most of it down in the Rio Hondo, only caught its fringes. Up this way you'd be right in the heart of it. The cattle'd die off like flies."

"They did," agreed the girl. "I remember old Sam

Veech laughing and boasting about selling out. He said he was real lucky, the books don't freeze."

With the boom of the cattle industry, eastern and foreign interests soughts to buy in on ranches. It had become the custom for such deals to be made with the range unseen, taking the stock figures from the outfit's concerned round-up tally books and accepting land office records to show how much land was involved. Most places on the western plains could be turned into successful ranching land and the system satisfied the buyers in most cases. While buying the book could profit the purchaser in a good year—when there would be many more cattle than shown in the tally book—taking over a ranch after a Texas blue.norther storm tore its way across the range, was disastrous. As the old rancher who sold to Stella Howkins had said, the books did not freeze; unfortunately, the same did not apply to the ranch's cattle.

"And she bought in right after the storm?" asked Danny.

"It broke the day the deal was completed."

"Whooee! I just bet she lost three-fifths of her stock."

"I think she did," the girl replied. "That could be why she started to take over the town, to try and regain her losses."

"Like I said, it'd hardly pay her for the effort," Danny objected. "How'd she get control here?"

"Through the storm. That blue norther did more than just kill off cattle. It almost wrecked the town. Then Tuttle arrived, just as we were thinking of pulling out and trying to make a start somewhere else, or starting to rebuild here. He said he was opening a bank in town. Oh, he was very helpful, loaning money to rebuild. Then we found out that he just about owned us body and soul. One family tried to run out. Their wagon came back empty, we found their bodies in a dried-out water course. A land-slide had done it, Kimble found at the inquest. Only nobody explained why the wagon came back instead of getting caught in the slide. After that things went slowly from bad to worse. Kimble had come in with Tuttle and took over the post office. Doctor Drager arrived, we needed a doctor here, our old one died in the storm. Boy, that Drager was an asset. As long as you behaved, you could have medical care. If you didn't—well, take Bescaby, his wife was sick and he'd been talking against Miss Howkins, refusing to borrow some more money from the bank to 'improve' his property. He learned that Drager would be busy for some time and couldn't visit. So Bescaby took the hint, borrowed the money and sank further into her hands. Drager arrived within an hour of Bescaby signing for the loan.''

"And Bescaby stood for it?" asked Danny.

"He stood for it."

"I figure there's getting on for a hundred grown men at least in this town," Danny went on. "Stella Howkins didn't have that many hired guns at first that your men couldn't have handled them."

"There's something you don't know," she replied. "You're in a town of cowards, Mr. Fog."

"How do you mean?"

"Not one man here fought in the War on either side."

"And that makes them cowards?"

"It does to most people. Bescaby was a professional pugilist, a rising young tophand from all accounts. Then he killed a man in the ring and refused to fight again. John Weaver, the blacksmith, I've seen him fell a mule with one hand, but I've also seen him mend a bird's broken wing. John wanted only to be left in peace. The rest, well some wouldn't fight in the War for religious reasons, others probably because they saw a chance to make money by staying out."

"And how'd you come into this?" asked Danny.

"Like the others, my folks came from Missouri. My father raised me, mother died when I was young. Dad was a happy man, he loved hunting, fishing, trailing a pack of hound-dogs. He was also a pretty good hotel keeper. Only we lived in Missouri and a man was expected to take the blue or the grey. Dad held no brief in

the slavery issue. He figured the Yankees used it to give
their supporters something to fight for. You know, free
those poor slaves. Only don't say what you aim to do
with them when they're freed, or think that most of
them were better off as slaves. And he didn't want to
support the southern states. So he refused to take sides.
After the War, his friends were all gone. Those who
fought for the South hated him as a Yankee, his
northern friends were too busy grabbing everything they
could from the rebels and regarded Dad as a reb.''

"It was a bad time for everybody.''

"I know,'' agreed Connie. "Dad gathered folks like
himself into a party and we moved south-west coming
into the cattle country of Texas. This was the only town
in a vast area. The cowhands accepted us for what we
were, not for what we had been. Oh, they played rough,
but they always paid for any damage they did and
nobody got hurt. Dad used to say they played hard
because they worked hard.''

"That's true enough,'' Danny put in. "Only I can't
see how not taking sides in the War makes your men
cowards.''

"Most people think it does. I doubt if there are more
than a dozens guns in town even. Even if there were,
could we fight against Stella Howkins when our first
move would bring immediate foreclosure of our notes at
the bank? Under the terms of the loans, Tuttle has the
right to demand payment in full within twenty-four
hours of giving notification.''

"You folks signed to that?'' Danny growled.

"It's all very well for you to talk!'' Connie snapped
hotly. "You didn't see the town, and you haven't heard
Tuttle talk. That man could charm a bird down out of a
tree. He seemed so jolly and helpful, and insisted that
the repayment clause was only put in for his stock-
holders' benefit. It would never be used, he told us.''

"Didn't put *that* into writing?''

"Of course not.''

"Hey gal, pull in your horns,'' Danny grinned,

looking about fifteen years old. "You're right, I haven't seen Tuttle at his best."

"You're a very nice man, Mr. Fog," the girl said.

"Then why not call me Danny?"

"I think I should tell you, I'm in love with Harvey Stackpole."

"Just my danged luck," Danny smiled. "Anyway, just try using my name, that Mr. Fog's making me feel awful old."

"How old are you?" Connie asked.

"Old enough to be a Ranger."

With her woman's instincts Connie realized she had touched a sore spot and guessed at its cause. Danny Fog lived in the shadow of his more famous brother and disliked mention being made about his age.

"Now *you* pull your horns in," she told him.

"Why didn't you get word to the local sheriff?" asked Danny, his good humour restored.

"Gale Gavin, the county sheriff's a politician as well as a lawman. He'd need certain proof before he'd move against somebody as powerful as Stella Howkins. And I think that one of his deputies takes pay from Howkins. Nobody dare chance it."

"Who took the letters to Carrintown for you?"

"The stage driver. Pedro can't keep an eye on me all the time and I managed to slip the driver the letters. He knows what's going on in town and helped."

"But why did you, I mean you personally write?"

For a long moment the girl did not reply, then she shrugged. "I've least to lose. We held a meeting, a few of us, and passed word around to the folks we can trust. Everybody agreed that we should try to bring in the Rangers."

"And you were the only one who dared write?"

"Let's say I had the best opportunity to get the letter out."

Danny let the matter drop. "Now I'm here, I'm damned if I know what I can do," he admitted. "Nobody would go into court and speak up against Miss

Howkins, even if I could find anything to arrest her for.
I could take her brother in for assault, but Bescaby
wouldn't sign the complaint. Apart from that, there's
nothing I can do."

Suddenly concern came to the girl's face. "Your life
is in danger all the time you're here," she gasped. "I
remember hearing Cheem tell Pedro what you did to
Harry Howkins. He's not used to being thwarted, his
sister gives him everything he asks for."

"Is that why you wear your hair like you do and dress
in that black frock?"

"Yes, Harry Howkins has an eye for the girls,"
agreed Connie, a hint of a blush growing on her cheeks.
It died and her face grew grim. "Statherm, the saddler,
had a pretty daughter. Howkins saw her at a dance, told
her to come riding with him the next day. She didn't go.
Two nights later she disappeared. They found her body
on the range by the Kiowa reservation, she'd been——"

"I can figure that part," Danny said gently.

"Wigg and two more of Howkins' men visited
Statherm and warned him what would happen if he tried
to blame Howkins for what the Kiowa obviously had
done. Then a dance-hall girl, pretty girl, found she was
having a baby and hinted Harry Howkins might be the
father. Two days later Wigg accused her of stealing his
wallet. He and his men tarred and feathered her, and
ran her out of town on a rail. After that Elliot, at the
saloon, received word not to employ any more girls and
get rid of the other four he had there."

"And you reckon Howkins might try for you?"

"I don't want to give him a reason," Connie said
soberly. "Harvey's a great artist, M—Danny, but he's
like the rest of the men in town. It's better that I never
know whether he would or wouldn't have the nerve to
fight for me."

"I reckon he might, only he's no fighting man."

"While I don't know much about you," she answered, "I'd match Harvey against you at wing-shooting
with a shotgun."

"Likely," Danny agreed. "Only there's a difference

in popping bob-white quail and tangling in a shooting match with professional gunhands like Wigg. I reckon Harvey'd try it for you—but I doubt if he'd walk away.''

"And you could?''

Danny shrugged. "I don't know if I could take Wigg," he admitted. "If I have to, I'll make a stab at it.''

The words recalled Connie's fear for Danny's safety. "Stella Howkins won't stand for you making her men look small the way you have been doing. I know why you're doing it.''

"I thought you took me for a lawman who just likes pushing folks around," he grinned.

"You certainly look and act that way," she countered. "But I know you're doing it to try to prove that Howkins' men aren't so terrible. It won't work. They've too tight a hold on the town. She could have you killed——''

"Not for a spell yet," Danny interrupted and told the girl of his deception.

"Do you think they believed it?" she asked.

"Tuttle got one of their men killed because of it. Feller called Furst, I'd had words with him earlier, laid for me when I left the saloon. Tuttle yelled a warning and I had to kill Furst.''

"It was Furst who tar-and-feathered the saloon girl.''

"He won't do it again," Danny drawled. "Say, where's your father?''

"He died in the blue norther.''

"I'm sorry.''

"It's all over now. But how long will you be safe?''

"Until she finds out for certain that there's no company of Rangers in Carrintown, by that time I hope Captain Jules'll have help on hand.''

"And if he doesn't?" Connie asked.

"I'm trying not to think of that," Danny replied. "Say, about those two fellers I mentioned. They did come?''

"Yes. Booked rooms and stayed for a week or so.

Then one night I came back from a visit and Pedro told me they had pulled out. I never thought anything about it though. Were they Rangers?"

"Mick Salmon and Pinky Pugh," Danny answered. "A brace of real good Rangers, and damned good friends.

"Didn't they send any word to your headquarters?"

"Not that we received. We don't go much for writing reports. But if they'd pulled out that long back, we ought to have heard from them by this time."

"Then you think——," Connie began.

"I don't think anything yet," Danny interrupted. "Tell me everything you can remember about them."

"There's not much."

"One of the smartest owlhoots in Texas was caught because he wore odd coloured socks. Sheriff saw them, went to tell the owlhoot; the feller figured the sheriff recognized him and grabbed for his gun. Only he was slow."

"You read that in a Ned Buntline book," the girl objected.

"Know the man who told Buntline the story. *He* didn't read it in any book," Danny answered. "Fact being, he was the sheriff—and my pappy."

"And what did all that lead up to?" Connie asked.

"Nothing's too small in law work. Think hard and tell me all you can."

"They rode in one day, just like any pair of drifting cowhands. Stella Howkins happened to be in town and they learned who she was, then asked her for a riding chore. When she refused, they let it be known that they aimed to stay around town for a time, until their money ran out."

"What'd they do?" Danny asked.

"Not much for the first week. Slept late in the morning, loafed on the porch out front until dark, then either drank a little or gambled at the saloon. They did take their horses and ride out a few times, just to get the bed-springs out, they said, but I don't know where they went."

"Wherever they went around here, they'd be on Lazy H land," Danny pointed out. "Say, how long has Greenwood been here?"

"He came in about three months ago, stayed a few days, hanging around town with Wigg. Then he disappeared, or at least, I didn't notice him around——"

The girl stopped speaking and stared hard at Danny.

"What's wrong?" he asked.

"The next time I saw him was the day he showed Pedro the Ranger's badge. And that was the morning after the two men left."

"Are you sure they left?" Danny growled.

"All their belongings had gone from their room and their account paid up. I never gave it a thought. Nobody would have guessed they were Rangers."

Danny did not reply. One man in town did not need to guess. Greenwood knew that Mick Salman and Pinky Pugh were Rangers.

## CHAPTER SIX

## We'll Raise Whatever Pay You Get

When arranging for the building of his bank, Tuttle demanded that his private office be given a window which overlooked Main Street. On the morning after Danny Fog arrived in Moondog, the banker sat at his desk and stared moodily through the window at the familiar scene. Ignoring the pile of papers awaiting his attention, Tuttle gave full rein to his thoughts. He did not like recent developments in town. First two Rangers arrived, now a third had come—one with reinforcements close at hand at that. Tuttle discounted Danny's story of the proposed bank robbery and knew he came in search of the first pair of Rangers.

For the first time since the early days of his stay in Moondog, Tuttle feared that things might go wrong with his employer's plans. Never one to underestimate any man, Tuttle saw Danny's true potential. The banker did not think Danny acted tough because of a bully's nature, but put it down to the real reason. Although Tuttle knew much about the town, he wondered if the Ranger's actions might give the local men courage to stand against the Lazy H. No man from the county sheriff's office could do so, but the Texas Rangers stood unique in their State's law enforcement organizations. They built their reputation the hard way and were anything but ignorant country hicks. Maybe the Rangers could stiffen the men of Moondog.

Chewing at the end of his pen, Tuttle threw a glance at the big safe fitted into the floor of his room. Inside lay only a portion of the bank's assets, the rest being held by Stella Howkins at the ranch house. However the banker's safe contained enough money to set him up comfortably should he be forced to make a run for his life. He wondered if a departure might be the best idea. Only it would need to be carefully planned. One slip, one hint of what he aimed to do, and death waited for him as surely as night followed day.

Turning his attention towards the window once more, Tuttle watched the few people who moved about the street, He began to realize how they felt, to know something of fear. The first two Rangers had come without anybody being aware of their position in life. When they disappeared a warning passed about not speaking of them sufficed to quell any curiosity the folks of the town might feel. Danny Fog would be different, for everybody knew him to be a Ranger.

Tuttle stiffened in his chair as he saw the object of his thoughts stroll out of the hotel. Carrying his saddle over one shoulder, Danny Fog walked along the opposite side of the street in the direction of the livery barn. An idea hit Tuttle, one so simple, he wondered why he failed to think of it before. Shoving back his chair he came to his feet. Just as he turned from the desk, a thought struck him. Opening the top drawer, he took out a handful of expensive cigars and thrust them into his vest pocket. Then he hurried out of his office, through the business section and on to the street.

Unaware of the interest he caused, Danny strolled along the sidewalk towards the livery barn. The previous night he and Connie talked for a long time, but without coming to any conclusions as to what lay behind Stella Howkins' domination of Moondog. Nor could Connie shed any light upon the disappearance of Salmon and Pugh. Until Danny told her, the girl had not even been aware that her roomers belonged to the Texas Rangers and she felt certain that none of the other townsfolk were better informed. All Connie knew for certain was that after the men disappeared Stella Howkins passed word for complete silence about them.

In Moondog Stella Howkins' words received obedience. The girl did say that the Lazy H men made a hurried round of the town shortly after Danny's arrival and gave an extra warning that nobody attempted to pass any information to him.

After finishing their talk, Danny escorted the girl downstairs. On checking, he found Pedro stretched upon the floor in a drunken stupor. Connie returned to her quarters without anyone other than Danny being aware of her disobedience to Stella Howkins' orders.

On rising that morning, Danny ate breakfast at the hotel. Pedro, sullen and showing signs of a bad hang-over, slouched in the background and watched Connie serve the food. For all he saw, he might just as well have stayed in the quiet of his room. With her back to the Mexican, Connie gave Danny a smile and a wink as she made as much of a clatter as possible. It took Danny all his strength of will to hold down a grin in return while watching Pedro's sufferings. One way and another Connie Hooper was proving to be quite a girl, Danny concluded. It almost seemed a pity that she had a sweetheart.

With breakfast over, Danny decided to make a start at searching the range. He did not know what he might find, but wished to get to know the lie of the land. Collecting his saddle and rifle from his room, he left the hotel. While strolling along the sidewalk, he made no attempt to stop and speak with anybody; but he noticed that some of the people did not appear quite so afraid to be seen near to him. Maybe his tactics were bearing fruit; he hoped so.

Tuttle also noticed the slight change in the citizens' attitude and knew that something must be done to nullify the Ranger's effect before it became too late. Forcing a jovial smile to his face, the banker fell alongside Danny.

"Good morning, Ranger," he greeted and dipped a hand into his jacket's breast pocket. "Have a cigar?"

"They're a mite too strong for a young feller like me," Danny replied, eyeing the long, black cigars in the silver case offered to him.

"I see you're going riding."

"Yep."

Ignoring the lack of cordiality in Danny's tones, Tuttle replaced his cigar-case and nodded in apparent approval. "That's good, I like to see a keen young lawman who gets on with his work."

"Always like to do my best," Danny answered.

"How do you like being a Ranger?" asked Tuttle, throwing a glance in Danny's direction.

"It's a living."

"You wouldn't want to resign?"

"I'd have to find another chore if I did."

"Well now," boomed Tuttle, "maybe I could help you there."

Watching the banker, Danny began to see how he managed to charm the townfolk into signing those damning mortgage notes when he offered them money. Tuttle oozed geniality, friendship and lack of guile, giving an appearance of bluff cordiality and helpfulness. All but his eyes that is. Danny read a warning in the man's watchful, unsmiling eyes.

"How?" asked Danny.

"You could take on here as town marshal."

"Could, huh?"

"Sure. There'd be mighty good pi——the pay'd be good."

Just in time Tuttle changed his words. Something told him that Danny was not the kind of man who would be interested in 'pickings' if he took on as town marshal.

"Pay's good in the Rangers," Danny pointed out.

"We'd raise whatever pay you get. I think we could go to a hundred and twenty-five and all found."

"That's a whole heap of money for a marshal in a town this size."

"We figure you'll earn it," Tuttle replied, then his voice took on a confidential note. "Quite frankly, our present marshal's not worth a cuss."

"I haven't seen him around much," Danny admitted.

"Nor will you. He's either getting drunk, too drunk

to walk, or sleeping it off on the office floor. This town could use a good, capable young man like you in charge of the law.''

"And you'd go to a hundred and twenty-five dollars a month?"

"Might even go higher," Tuttle answered and another thought struck him.

If he could persuade Danny to take over the law, there might be a chance of cutting Stella Howkins out of the game. With a good man wearing the law badge, one who had already proved himself unafraid of the Lazy H's hired killers, Tuttle figured he could remove Stella Howkins and have the town for himself. From the way the Ranger mentioned his proposed salary, he might be considering the offer.

"How much higher?" asked Danny.

"One fifty," replied Tuttle, almost holding his breath as he waited for the answer. When none came, he continued, "That's more than you make as a Ranger."

"Why sure," Danny agreed.

Despite the fact that they handled some of the most dangerous outlaws in the West, and that they bore the responsibility of policing the thousands of miles which formed Texas, the Rangers drew only eighty to a hundred dollars a month in pay. A top gunhand, among the West's best paid professions, could pull down a hundred and fifty dollars or more. Knowing that, Danny decided that his tactics since arriving must be meeting with some success. The banker offered him top fighting man's wages to change sides. Of course, there would be one thing to remember—even if Danny thought of taking the offer—once he resigned from the Rangers, he was Stella Howkins' man, or dead.

Not that Danny intended to accept. In his time as a Ranger, he had received other such offers, although few came as high as Tuttle's suggestion. Danny decided to play along for a spell and see just how eager the other man might be.

"How about it then?" the banker inquired.

"There's a lot to being a Ranger," Danny replied. "It gives a man something that other peace officers don't have."

Which was true enough. A Texas Ranger's jurisdictional powers covered the whole of the Lone Star State. Unlike a town marshal, whose powers ended at the city limits; or a sheriff, who was confined to the boundaries of his county; a Ranger could come and go anywhere within the State. A United States marshal—far different from a town marshal, who was merely a municipal police officer—could only investigate Federal offences, but a Ranger had the right to look into any infraction of the laws of the State of Texas. Wealth, social and political position meant nothing to a Ranger; he took orders from his captain, who, in turn, was answerable only to the Governor. So any man who gained entrance to the Rangers could claim to be a person of some consequence in Texas.

(It is interesting to note that through its eighty or more years of operation the Texas Rangers had far less cases of dishonesty amongst its members than any other law enforcement body in the United States).

Considering Danny's words, Tuttle nodded in agreement. Then he said, "Sure it does. Longer hours of duty. Days in the saddle. No chance of settling down in one place and making a home. Here you'd be settled in a comfortable place, making good money, and without much danger."

"You're making it sound mighty interesting," Danny admitted.

By the time they had reached the livery barn and walked through its open doors. Seeing Bescaby cleaning one of the stalls, Tuttle decided to make sure the man knew his chances of Ranger salvation had gone.

"Then you're going to take my offer and be our town marshal, Ranger?" Tuttle boomed in a carrying voice.

Danny saw Bescaby's head jerk up and for a moment their eyes met. Misery and hopelessness showed on the livery barn owner's face. After one brief look. Bescaby turned his attention back to his work.

"I didn't say that," Danny answered Tuttle in just as carrying a voice.

Once more Bescaby glanced Danny's way and a faint glow of hope came to the fight-scarred face.

Only by an effort did Tuttle restrain the angry exclamation that rose. He wanted to drive out the tiny flicker of hope Bescaby might be feeling before it took too firm a hold, and figured showing the man that Danny had come over to the Lazy H would do so.

"It's a mighty good offer," the banker pointed out. "You won't get another as good."

"Likely," Danny agreed. "But I'm happy enough as a Ranger. That way I've only one boss and I don't have to watch whose toes I tread on."

"I see!" growled the banker, fighting to retain his genial smile and failing by a good country mile.

Having thought Danny seriously considered his offer, the banker now wondered if the young Ranger merely played with him. However, Danny gave him no chance to reopen the subject. Entering the *sabino's* stall, Danny started to fuss with his mount. For a moment he thought that Tuttle would be foolish enough to follow him. The banker stood scowling at Danny's back, then took a step towards the open door of the stall. Instantly the *sabino* let out an explosive snort, sounding as mean as a winter-starved grizzly bear, and turned its head, ears flattening down in warning.

Taking a hurried step to the rear, the banker yelped, "Watch that horse!"

"Shucks," Danny replied calmly. "He won't hurt *me*."

Once more the anger glowed in Tuttle's eyes. He turned to Bescaby who stood watching everything that happened.

"Have my horse saddled in twenty minutes," he ordered.

"Sure, Mr. Tuttle," the barn's owner replied.

"You won't change your mind about my offer, Ranger?" the banker asked.

"Nope. I'm happy enough as I am."

Without another word, Tuttle turned and stamped from the barn. Outside he looked both ways along the street in the hope of seeing either Kimble or Drager, but could find no sign of them. Nor did there appear to be any of the Lazy H hardcases in sight and who could have been pressed into service to watch the Ranger while he was left with Bescaby. If it had not been for the urgency of the situation, Tuttle would have stayed in the barn until Danny left. However, Tuttle wanted to reach his boss and tell her of his attempted bribery. Stella Howkins would not like it; she hated failure. Thinking of the fury she showed when other things went wrong, Tuttle wondered if he should tell her of his failure, then decided he had better do so. If she heard of it second-hand her fury would be that much the worse; and Tuttle knew either Drager or Kimble would be only too pleased to tell her, should they learn.

Much as he disliked the thought of leaving Danny alone with Bescaby, Tuttle could see no way of avoiding it. After the incident with Bescaby's sick wife, the banker doubted if the other would dare speak out of turn, even while alone. So Tuttle strode off in the direction of his home, wanting to change into clothes more suitable for riding a horse.

In the livery barn, Danny prepared for a day's hard riding. He wanted to see as much of the Lazy H range as possible that day. Of course he would be unable to cover all Stella Howkins' holdings in one day, but wanted to see the area around the ranch if possible. As always, his first thought were for the welfare of the big *sabino*. His life might depend on the horse's condition and he wanted to take no chances. From the appearance of the stall, Bescaby had attended to the *sabino's* welfare that morning and the horse looked ready to go.

While Danny worked, Bescaby stood in the next stall, a pitchfork in his hands and a thoughtful expression on his face. He darted several glances at the open doors, seemed on the verge of speaking twice, but did not. At last he ran the tip of his tongue across his lips and came to a decision.

"About those two fellers, Ranger," he began in a low voice, darting worried looks at the doors.

"How about them?" Danny answered, his voice no louder than the other man's, without turning to the speaker. "Were they here?"

"For a spell. At least there was two of them here, one rode a washy bay, the other a dun with white legs."

Danny had often noticed how different people noticed varying things when asked for a description. While Connie at the hotel described the men's physical features, Bescaby mentioned the colour of their horses first.

"That's them," Danny agreed.

"They came in about three weeks back, left their hosses at the barn here for maybe a week or so, then left."

"Did you see them go?" Danny asked.

Before Bescaby could answer, a shadow fell across the doorway. Instantly the barn's owner swung away from Danny and gave his attention to forking the straw on the floor of the stall. Danny gave just as careful attention to the state of his *sabino's* near fore hoof. The owner of the shadow proved to be a hurrying townsman who passed by without a glance into the barn. Even if he had chanced to look, he would have seen nothing to tell him that Bescaby went against Stella Howkins' orders.

Having once gained the courage to defy the boss of the Lazy H, Bescaby appeared to be ready to cooperate with Danny. After the passerby disappeared from sight, Bescaby turned his head towards Danny once more and continued:

"I didn't see them leave. They rode out one morning, left their saddlebags with me. That night Wigg and a couple more Lazy H men rode into town and came here. They told me the two men had sent them in to collect their belongings. Saw they'd already got the fellers' bedrolls, and I handed over the saddlebags. Then Wigg paid me what the fellers owed me for the keep of their hosses. That surprised me. Lazy H don't often pay for anything they take."

"And you never saw them again?" asked Danny.

"No. Wigg and his men passed word that nobody had to speak about the two men. Say, are they badly wanted?"

"No."

"But you said——"

"That was a blind. They were my friends, and a couple of Rangers."

"They never said——" Bescaby began.

"They weren't likely to go around shouting it from the roofs," Danny interrupted. "If Greenwood hadn't told his boss I was one, I'd not have said I belonged to the Rangers either."

The words seemed to have little effect on Bescaby. "So the Rangers came after all," he said, more to himself than to Danny. "When we didn't hear anything after Connie's first letter, we figured that Stella Howkins had fixed it so the Rangers wouldn't come in to help us."

"Mister," Danny growled, his voice deep and angry. "Nobody buys off a Ranger investigation, or gets it called off either."

"No offence, Ranger," Bescaby apologized. "Only the way things are here, we all think that she can do anything she wants."

"My uncle, Ole Devil Hardin, owns a spread twice as big as the Lazy H. He's a real good friend of Governor Howard, Captains Murat, McDonald and Beldon. But even Uncle Devil couldn't pull enough to stop a Ranger doing his duty."

"We didn't know that. What do you aim to do now?"

"Nose around, learn all I can. Keep shoving the Lazy H hard-cases around to show you folks that they aren't tough enough to chew iron and spit rust—and wait."

"Wait?" repeated Bescaby just a touch suspiciously. After a year of living in fear, he mistrusted everybody.

"Wait," agreed Danny. "I'm not scared, but I'm not *loco* either. Rough-handling her ordinary hands is one thing. Stacking up alone against maybe forty hired guns comes out something a little mite different. One lone man can't face those kind of odds and walk out of the game alive.''

"We're not fighting men here," Bescaby stated.

"That's for sure," Danny grunted. "But there'll be help on its way soon. I don't reckon Stella Howkins' men'll be willing to tangle in a shooting match with a bunch of Rangers. Some of them might, but not many.''

"I wish we could do something to help you," Bescaby remarked.

"You can," Danny said.

"What?"

"Just carry on acting like you have ever since my arrival. No matter how you get to feeling, don't show any change to the Lazy H.''

"I won't and I'll see that word gets passed around for the others to do the same.''

While talking, Danny had continued saddling his horse. He led the *sabino* from the stall. Just as he was about to mount, a thought struck him and he looked at Bescaby.

"Where'd you reckon Tuttle'll be riding to when he comes for his horse?''

"Out to the Lazy H.''

"Figured that myself. Say, how'd I get to the Lazy H house?''

"Follow the stage trail north-west, about three miles out of town you'll find a track leading off——''

"Only one thing being I want to get there without being seen.''

"Then you'd best cut across the range, follow the rim along the Moondog Creek and you'll soon find the house.''

"I'll do just that," grinned Danny.

Swinging into his saddle, he rode the *sabino* from the barn. If Bescaby's attitude be anything to go on, Danny's plan for building up the courage and confidence was starting to show results.

## CHAPTER SEVEN

## I've Seen You Before

Holding his big *sabino* to a steady walk, Danny Fog rode along the bottom of the valley, heading for a small clump of trees that he decided ought to hold some cattle as it offered shade and shelter grazing animals sought. He rode warily, with many darting glances at the rims above him and to his rear. Since coming on to the Lazy H range, he had tried to keep to low land and only allowed himself to be lined against the sky after he first checked carefully that nobody would see him.

Before joining the Rangers, Danny received instruction in the art of unseen travel through potentially dangerous country. His teacher, the Ysabel Kid, learned such things from his Comanche grandfather,* and passed on much wisdom that Danny found invaluable when working on a Ranger chore.

After only a short time upon the Lazy H, Danny became aware, despite the good grazing and water, of a lack of domesticated animal life. In two hours of searching, however, he saw a big Texas grizzly bear, a couple of foraging black bears, one small bunch of Texas grey wolves, and a cougar. This latter surprised Danny, who had a good knowledge of wild animals, for it proved to be a medium-sized, pale tawny coloured cat, such as one saw in the Sierra Madre country but which was replaced by the larger, more greyish-hued cougar in Texas.

* Told in COMANCHE

The numerous skeletons of storm-killed cattle explained the unusual concentration of carnivorous animals on the Lazy H range; most likely the Sierra Madre cougar and the other animals fed their way across the range in the path of the big Blue Norther storm, living on the weather's bounty. From what Danny saw, Stella Howkins appeared to have a fair-sized predator-control chore on her hands in addition to her other problems. By this time the last of the storm-killed food had been finished and the bears, wolves and cougar would play havoc among any new stock the Lazy H brought in.

Danny started thinking about Stella Howkins' stock problem when he left town and decided to try to form an idea of what her losses during the storm had been. In a short time he learned that the losses must have been enormous, for skeletons dotted the range and were piled up in one place, where a small bunch of cattle had crowded and huddled together in the hope of avoiding the fury of the elements.

Using the skill and knowledge gained as a boy riding the OD Connected range, Danny sought out possible spots where cattle would gather. Although he found a few small bunches, few of the animals bore just the Lazy H brand. The rest all had been counter-branded; a line burned across the original mark of ownership to nullify it and the Lazy H's sign placed alongside the first brand. Counter-branding was legal enough, provided the original owner performed the operation.

Another thing struck Danny. Stella Howkins appeared to be stocking her range with mature cattle. A sound scheme—for such stock would have grown through the ailments which killed so many calves—but expensive. With cattle commanding good prices at the Kansas railheads, most Texas ranchers preferred to drive their stock north rather than sell it locally. Possibly Stella used her undeniable charm to talk various ranchers into selling her small numbers of cattle as basis for a new Lazy H herd. In fact, many ranchers would be willing to do so, even without her exercising any charm.

Even as he rode towards the grove, Danny heard sounds beyond the next rim. Many hooves pounded the ground and cattle bellowed, the sounds of a herd on the move. Ignoring the clump of trees, Danny rode towards the sound. He covered two miles before he came in sight of the cattle. Keeping in cover, he topped a rim and looked down to where a group of five men herded about a hundred head of cattle down a valley bottom.

From his place, Danny studied the approaching herd. All appeared to be prime grown animals, cows, heifers and young bulls. The men handling the herd were tough looking, wary and well-armed, led by a lean, bearded hard-case Danny thought he ought to know.

Ignoring the men for a moment, Danny turned his eyes to the cattle, but they passed with their left flanks to him and cattle always wore their mark of ownership on the right. Danny wanted to learn what brands the cattle carried. So he swung his *sabino*, meaning to keep under cover, ride out of sight, cut around, halt in a position where he could see and read the brands. He reckoned without the alertness of one of the herd's handlers. The instant Danny moved, the man whirled his head around and reached for a gun.

"Packey!" he yelled. "Up there!"

Swinging his horse from its position at that point, the bearded man also looked and reached his hand gunwards. Neither fired, even though they drew their weapons, for shooting off guns around a herd of moving cattle was a good way of starting a stampede.

Finding himself observed, Danny decided to try a daring bluff. By that time Stella Howkins would have ordered her men not to kill Danny until she checked on his story about the Rangers in Carrintown. So he figured he would be safe enough riding down and taking a closer look at the cattle, under the pretence of asking about signs of outlaws who were supposed to be coming to rob the bank.

Gun in hand, the man called Packey rode up the slope towards Danny. The other four allowed the cattle to slow down and halt, then all turned their eyes in the direction of their leader as he halted his horse facing Danny.

"Put that away," Danny ordered, glancing at the gun. "Miss Howkins wouldn't like it if you shot me."

Much to his surprise, a grin creased Packey's face and the gun went away.

"Shucks, whyn't you shout that you rode for the Lazy H?" asked the bearded man. "Gave me and the boys a turn, coming out on us like that."

Which meant the quintet did not work for the Lazy H. Nor were they stealing the ranch's cattle or Packey's greeting would have been less cordial. Apparently, Packey took Danny for a member of Stella Howkins' crew. Danny saw his chance and intended to make the most of it by learning all he could from the bearded man.

"I didn't come up on you anyways, except that I had to come over that rim to get to this side," Danny told Packey, his voice truculent and tough.

Packey's eyes went to Danny's face, a slight frown creeping to the bearded lips. For a moment Danny thought the other would take exception to his words then a puzzled glint came to Packey's eyes and he dropped his gaze first to Danny's guns, then to the *sabino*.

"I've seen you before someplace," the bearded man stated.

"Likely," agreed Danny. "I've been there."

"Where?"

"Someplace."

"Which place?" growled Packey.

"Most any place you care to name. I've been around. Likewise, don't like nosey cusses asking questions."

Again the scowl came to Packey's eyes as they met Danny's mocking stare. Danny lounged in his saddle, cold contempt showing in every inch of his body. In almost every detail he looked like a tough young hard-case, a professionel fighting man supremely confident in his own ability to handle the man he faced. His pose seemed to satisfy Packey and quell any objections the other might have.

"Where-at's the house?" asked Packey, forcing through a smile about as friendly as the grin on a skull.

During his time on the Lazy H land, Danny had found a high point, from the top of which he could study the surrounding ranges. While up there he located the ranch's main buildings and so was in a position to answer Packey's question without arousing the other's suspicions.

"Just keep 'em pointed as you are now. When you hit the creek about two miles on, follow it along. You'll come to the house that ways."

"Thought you'd come to meet us," Packey said suspiciously.

"You thought it. I didn't say it. I'm handling something for the boss," Danny answered. "Don't reckon she figured you'd need a wet-nurse to find the house."

Once again Packey forced through a smile. He studied Danny's handsome face and reached a conclusion. A young cuss like that might have worked his way into the boss lady's favour *real* good. Making fuss with him would not tend to create harmony or good will with Stella Howkins; and Packey was aware of the value of good relations in the conducting of business matters. So he ignored the mocking jibes of the tall young man until he knew better how the other stood with the owner of the Lazy H.

"What's this Howkins gal like?" he asked, signalling his men to continue the drive.

"Quite a looker. Only happen you want to keep your face whole, don't go calling her anything but Miss Howkins when you meet her."

"She's like that, huh?" grunted Packey.

"Try talking out of turn and you'll see. Let's take a look at the herd."

Side-by-side they rode down the slope, past the line

of moving cattle and watchful men. Packey expected Danny to slow down when they reached the point of the herd, but the Ranger carried on riding, swinging across the path of the herd and halting the *sabino* on the right flank of the approaching animals.

First thing to strike Danny as the animals moved by was that they carried a variety of vented brands. Secondly, he saw that the counter-branding had been done when an animal was found wrongly marked, or if a branded animal was sold. None of the animals had been wrongly branded, for they showed only the vented brand and the Lazy H. No rancher would counter-brand his stock unless ready to ship them, for the animal so treated could be picked up and given another brand by anybody who happened to find it.

Then Danny remembered one occasion when cattle would be counter-branded and left without any other sign of ownership.

"Fine bunch of cattle," he remarked, searching for a way to gain the necessary information.

"Sure. Too damned good for filling the bellies of a bunch of stinking Kiowa bucks."

Danny held down any feelings the words might have brought, for he had proved his theory with little or no trouble. When buying cattle to feed the reservation-held Indians, it had become the Bureau of Indian Affairs' policy to choose a time of low prices. Buying agents collected and had counterbranded numbers of cattle which were held on government grazing land until needed to feed the Indians. At least two of the passing cattle showed faint signs of burning that the Lazy H could not entirely hide. Danny guessed that the cattle had been hair branded; had the government's brand burned only in the hair and not upon the skin so that when the winter coat grew out the animal carried only the vented brand of its original owner. After that the cattle could have another brand burned on their hide, turning them into what for all intents and purposes were legally-bought stock.

"Took us a hell of a time to brand them," Packey

complained, cutting through Danny's thoughts. "I don't see why it couldn't have been done here."

"You'll get paid for it," Danny replied unsympathetically.

Although he did not mention it, Danny could guess at why Stella Howkins requested that the branding be done before the herd reached her property. Although the Kiowa reservation bordered Stella Howkins' west boundary line, the nearest government grazing lay on the western side of the reservation. Packey and his bunch could not chance driving across the reservation, and anybody herding cattle which bore only a vented brand and no other sign would attract attention. Having the herd counter-branded with the Lazy H gave the men an answer to any questioner who had the backing to give him the right to ask; the herd belonged to Stella Howkins, who bought it as part of her re-stocking plan for the Lazy H.

Even if he had not guessed it before, Danny began to see now that Stella Howkins was a mighty smart and keen business woman. It would take a hell of a lot of proving that she bought the animals knowing they had been stolen once they mingled with her other cattle.

"Sure we get paid for it," Packey agreed.

"Get a good price, too," Danny guessed.

"More'n we'd get most places," the bearded man admitted. "Twenty bucks a head."

While working against the cow thieves of Caspar County, Danny had learned more than a little about the illegal business. He knew the comparatively low prices paid for stolen stock. If a cow thief made ten dollars a head, he could count himself very lucky. Operating the way she did, Stella Howkins could double that price and still show a considerable profit.

"You've got no cause for complaint then," Danny stated.

"Me?" answered Packey. "Naw! Anyways, Greenwood told me what to expect if I took on to work for her. Say, that Howkins gal must be something if she has Rangers working for her."

Only just in time did Danny bite down on his angry denial as it rose automatically. To burst out with a statement that Greenwood no longer belonged to the Rangers would not be in keeping with his pose as a hired gunhand.

Danny realized he had solved one of the problems, how Stella Howkins managed to locate and hire cow thieves. With knowledge gained in the Rangers, Greenwood had the means of contacting cow thieves and spreading word of the potential market Lazy H offered for stolen goods which had been suitably treated. Cold fury filled Danny, although he tried to hold it down. He swore that he would either arrest or kill Greenwood for betraying the oath taken when enlisting in the Rangers and bringing disrepute on that fine organization. Danny felt all the bitter anger and hatred of an honest lawman confronted by another peace officer gone bad. Previously there had been no proof that Greenwood did more than take fighting pay from the Lazy H. Now Danny knew the other used his Ranger's knowledge for illegal purposes. No Ranger would show any mercy on another of the organization who had gone bad.

Forcing himself to control his feelings, Danny answered Packey's statement.

"She's mighty slick all right."

"We'll push on in. You coming with us?"

"Nope. She sent me out to scout the Kiowa reservation line."

"You're a mite off course," Packey said suspiciously.

"Maybe, only don't you try pushing it," Danny snapped back. "And don't you go blabbing it to her that you've seen me on the way to town. She don't take kindly to the hired help wasting time she's paid for."

A grin twisted the bearded lips and Packey decided that the young man could not be that deep in Stella Howkins' favour after all.

"Sounds like she's got you buffaloed," he said.

"Maybe she has, maybe she ain't," growled Danny. "One thing I do know. Anybody who crosses her winds up wolfbait, and I'm too young to want to die. So happen you let slip you've seen me out this ways, I'll call you a liar and spit right in your face.''

In Texas no man called another a liar unless ready to back the words with a smoking gun, and spitting in another's face was the supreme insult. Packey could see that the young man did not intend to allow Stella Howkins to learn that he failed to obey her orders. While following the dangerous profession of cow thief —with a rope very properly awaiting him on capture— Packey could not claim to be good with a gun. His every instinct told him that he would need to be real good to take the tough-looking blond cuss and come through alive.

A conciliatory expression came to Packey's face and he held out a hand in a peace sign.

"Take it easy, friend," he said. "Ain't no call at all to go off half-cocked about it. Reckon old Packey Pawson knows the signs. Bet there's a gal in town who's a danged sight more interesting than riding the Kiowa line.''

"Sure is. Right pretty gal too. Only St—Miss Howkins don't know nothing about her.''

Danny gave the other a confidential wink. While talking, he had been conscious of the other's scrutiny and guessed at the thoughts Packey reached. From the sly grin the other showed, Danny saw he had made a meat-in-the-pot hit. Packey had decided that Danny was *real* close to Stella and not in a professional capacity. The last words were designed to strengthen Packey's belief, and also give a much stronger reason for Danny's desire that Stella did not learn of his presence so far from his appointed place of duty.

"Say, what's she got against Kiowas?" Packey inquired.

"Huh?" asked Danny, stopping his horse as he began to turn it from the man.

"Greenwood told us that if we saw any of them on the Lazy H, Miss Howkins'd likely give us a bonus for their scalps.''

"She just don't like Injuns, I reckon," Danny replied, wanting to get away before Packey started wondering why he rode over to check on the herd when his only intention should have been to stay out of sight.

Apparently the thought had not reached Packey and he appeared to accept hatred of Indians as the reason for the bounty offer.

"Well, I'll get after my boys," Packey stated.

"And I'll get on my way," Danny answered. "You mind what I said now."

"It'll cost you a bottle of Old Stump Blaster," grinned Packey. "Hope that gal in town's worth it."

"She will be," Danny replied with a wink. "She sure will be."

Packey watched Danny ride off in the direction from which he came, then gave a low chuckle and swung his horse in the direction of his herd. Galloping the horse, he caught up alongside the nearest of his men.

"You ever see that young cuss afore, Alf?" he asked.

"Nope. Seen plenty like him though. Hard young cuss, fast with a gun and don't like work."

"That's how I read him," agreed Packey.

"From what I've heard that's the only sort Stella Howkins hires," Alf commented. "What's he doing out this ways?"

"Gone to see his gal in town when he should be working."

"For shame, and him drawing p——"

"You keep your lip buttoned when we get to the Lazy H house," Packey cut in on Alf's levity. "Don't let on we've seen him, not unless you want your head blowed clean off."

After explaining to Alf the reason for his silence, Packey visited each of his men in turn and passed on the warning. Knowing their leader to be a capable man in his own right, they all decided that silence was golden in the matter of the tall blond visitor's presence at the herd.

Once clear of the herd, Danny halted his *sabino* and

gave rapid thought to the new developments. He hoped
his threat would prevent Packey's bunch mentioning
seeing him when they reached the ranch. If Stella
Howkins heard how much he learned from Packey, she
would want him dead. Danny now knew a whole lot too
much for her safety and continued liberty. Even his
bluff about Ranger support in Carrintown might no
longer hold her back from trying to silence him.

Deciding he had done enough for one day, Danny
pointed his horse in the direction of Moondog. While
still retaining his caution, he let the *sabino* make better
time. If he must make a fight for his life, he wanted to
do it in town, where he might possibly receive aid from
the citizens.

Three miles fell behind him and a crashing in some
near-by bushes sent his right hand stabbing to the off-
side Colt. He did not draw the weapon, for a big
longhorn bull burst into sight and went barrelling off at
a good speed across the range ahead of him.

Suddenly a big, shaggy brown shape lurched into
sight among a clump of blueberry bushes in the bull's
path. Danny saw the bull make a frenzied attempt to
swing aside. Then a powerful foreleg, tipped by long,
steel-hard, razor-sharp claws, drove downwards. The
bull's head snapped to one side under the impact of the
blow, and even from where he sat Danny heard bones
pop. The bull buckled up and went crashing to the
ground and its killer, the grizzly bear Danny saw earlier,
moved forward.

Instantly Danny brought his snorting, scared *sabino*
to a halt. Bending forward, he jerked free the Winchester from its boot. Even with it in his hands, he made
no attempt to shoot. A man did not tangle with a full-
grown member of the Texas flat-headed grizzly bear
family when armed with only a Winchester Model '66
rifle unless cornered with no way out. While the
repeating rifle could not be equalled in its class, it had
never been built to meet the needs of handling *Ursus
texensis texensis* at close range. While the rifle could kill

a grizzly, Danny knew that the slightest mistake in his aim could wind him up on the ground, with the bear sitting on his chest and eating his face.

The bull was undoubtedly dead and nothing Danny did would alter that. Nor did he feel that Stella Howkins rated his aid in clearing her range of predators. So, as the grizzly swung its head towards him, Danny kneed his horse into movement, turned it from its original course and rode a wide circle around the bear.

For a few moments the grizzly stood with its forepaws on the quivering sides of its victim, snarling a challenge and watching the departing Danny. Then it settled down to feed on the still warm flesh of the dead bull.

## CHAPTER EIGHT

## I Want That Ranger Dead

While the big Blue Norther storm wreaked havoc across the range country and did considerable damage to Moondog, among other towns, it failed to make any impression on the Lazy H ranch house. Erected in the days of the Spanish-Mexican occupation of Texas, the house had been built to withstand any storm. The house stood in the centre of a large valley, sheltered from the elements by bush and tree-dotted slopes on all sides for the valley made a large curve at that point.

Standing in the porch, Stella Howkins watched Tuttle ride towards her. As always when outside the house and in its grounds, she felt that she was being watched, that hostile eyes studied her every move. Ignoring Tuttle's approaching form, she turned and scanned the slopes of the valley, hoping to catch just one sight of the watchers. She saw nothing human, only the familiar slopes of her home ranges. On several occasions almost every man of her crew rode out to scour the slopes thoroughly, but without result. The watchers withdrew at the first warning of a search and left no sign of their going. Of course she knew the identity of the watchers and was fully aware of the cause of that unceasing observation. That was one reason she never allowed all her men to be off the place at one time, but always retained at least half-a-dozen of the hands around the house.

By the time Stella had concluded her fruitless scanning of the surrounding range, Tuttle reached the porch and dismounted. He tied his horse to the hitching rail and walked to where Stella stood waiting.

"Good afternoon, Miss Howkins," he greeted.

"Good afternoon, Tuttle," she replied. "What brings you here?"

Until that moment Tuttle had never realized just how much he disliked the woman's attitude. Never once had she addressed him as 'mister,' or in any way treated him as a social equal and an important factor in the successful completion of her plans—whatever they may be. Tuttle suddenly realized that he knew little of the actual plans, or what lay behind Stella Howkins' actions. After a year of working together he felt he deserved more consideration that that accorded to him. Without his running of the bank, she could do——an uneasy recollection interrupted his indignant thoughts. While Stella Howkins put him in charge of the bank, every move he made had been planned by her, every detail arranged for him. Unpalatable as the thought might be, Stella Howkins not only could do without him, but she held information capable of sending him to jail for a long time. Not that she would be likely to use that information, although it had been very useful to secure his services. If he crossed her, it would be a bullet that removed his threat, not a jail sentence, Stella Howkins firmly believed that dead men told no tales.

"I thought you might like to hear what's happening in town," he said, putting aside his discontent and speaking in a friendly manner.

"Then you'd better come in and tell me."

With that Stella turned and walked back into the house. Tuttle followed the woman, scowling at her back. They crossed the hall and entered the sitting room. After waving the banker into a chair, Stella walked to the big windows and looked out past where Tuttle's horse stood and across the open land to the slopes. Almost a minute passed, with her standing and ignoring the man.

"You heard about last night?" Tuttle finally said,

and realized that it always fell on him to open the speaking.

"All about it," she agreed.

"I acted for the best. The way those fools in the bar behaved, Fog would have known something was wrong."

"Of course," Stella purred.

Her cold, unwinking stare unnerved Tuttle. Often before he had met her he determined to force a change in her attitude towards him, and failed when her cold eyes bored into him. At that moment he could not tell whether she approved or disapproved of his actions the previous night, so he sought to further clear himself of any blame.

"Outside the saloon," he said hurriedly, "I had to warn the Ranger." He ran his tongue over his lips. "There just wasn't anything else to do. I didn't know if Fog told me the truth about——"

"You did the right thing," Stella put in.

"I had to think fast. There wasn't time to explain to Furst."

"Furst was a fool, and he died through his folly. I can hire a dozen to replace him."

Confidence began to rise in Tuttle again. "How're the men taking it?" he asked. "About my warning the Ranger?"

"How should they take it?" Stella sniffed. "I'm splitting Furst's pay and property between them, they don't care. Especially as I explained why you acted as you did."

"It looks like the Ranger hasn't got anywhere in town," Tuttle remarked, after a brief pause.

"You might be a shade premature in that," she answered. "Have you seen him today?"

"Early this morning. He was thinking of taking a ride on your ranges. In fact he left. I'd have followed him——"

"Stick to the banking and leave that kind of work to somebody who could do it properly," Stella told him mockingly. "Fog would have seen you before you followed him half a mile. Anyway, let him ride across the ranges, he'll find nothing."

"I suppose not," agreed Tuttle.

"I *know* not!" she snapped. "You said you saw him this morning, what did you talk about?"

"I—I made him an offer."

"What kind of offer?"

"I suggested he resigned from the Rangers and became Moondog's town marshal."

"And he refused," Stella smiled, only it was not a humour-filled or friendly smile.

"I went to a hundred and twenty-five dollars a month and found."

"You could have offered him a half-share in all I make," Stella replied, "and the answer would still be 'no'."

"Everybody has his price!" Tuttle sniffed.

"So you thought when you bilked my dear uncle's company and tried to bribe that book-keeper," Stella reminded him. "Only he came straight to—well, luckily he came to me first, or you'd be in jail now."

"You don't have to remind me!" he snapped.

"Oh yes I do," she answered. "Otherwise you might get the wrong idea. You have a lot of wrong ideas, Tuttle. Attempting to bribe Fog was one. A man like him doesn't become a Ranger for the money it brings him. Making an attempt like you did only lets him know that there's something wrong in town."

"Do you believe his story?" asked the man, fighting down his anger at her mocking words.

"About coming to be on hand when the bank robbery takes place?"

"That and sending word to Carrintown every night."

"I don't believe the first. He came to look for the other two Rangers."

"And the other?" asked Tuttle worriedly.

"Now there you have a point," she said. "It's unlikely that Murat would send in a lone man when two others had disappeared, unless he was able to get help to his man quickly.''

"Is there any way we can check with Carrintown?''

"I have already checked, but haven't received any answer yet. Depending on what I hear, I'll know how to handle Mr. Fog.''

"What does Greenwood think?'' Tuttle inquired, ignoring the emphasis Stella placed on the first 'I' of her reply.

"I just told you what Greenwood thinks,'' she replied. "If Fog left town so early, how is it you only just came to tell me about it?''

"I'd have been here sooner, but the horse Bescaby gave me threw a shoe and I had to walk back with it. Then I found that he'd taken all the other horses out to range-graze them. So I went to the blacksmith's shop and Weaver wasn't there. When I found him, it took time for him to shoe the horse.''

"Quite a series of mishaps,'' purred Stella.

"If they were mishaps,'' Tuttle pointed out.

"Why must you always say the obvious?'' she groaned. "My dear uncle always used to say that when there was nothing foolish left to say, he could rely upon you to say it.''

"Your uncle——!'' began Tuttle hotly.

"There's nothing original you could say about him that I haven't already thought and said!'' she interrupted and her face for once showed expression, twisting into bitter, hate-filled lines. With an effort she mastered her emotions and turned her eyes back to the banker. "Coincidences do happen. Horses throw shoes, I believe a battle was lost through one doing so. Bescaby range-grazes his stock regularly, and Johnny Weaver doesn't spend every hour of the day in his shop.''

"Yes, but——''

"You're doing it again,'' she snapped. "You're going to say, but they don't all happen together usually. It's strange that they should on the day after a Ranger comes into town and starts rough-handling my men.''

"Then we ought to——"

Yet again Stella cut across the banker's words, finishing them halfway through their course. "I've noticed a tendency with you so say 'we' as if you're in partnership with me."

"I think that after all I've done for you that I might be entitled to some consideration!" Tuttle replied.

"You do for me only what your past indiscretions force you to do. I need you only because of the idiotic prejudice which insists a woman's place is as a slave in the home. You are a figure-head, no more, no less. Any time you feel differently, let me know."

Cold eyes glared at Tuttle and the courage which rose sparked out again. Before he could say another word, there came a further interruption. Stella's brother came slouching through the door, a mocking sneer on his face. From his attitude, it was plain that he had been indulging in his usual habit of eavesdropping. Halting at his sister's side, he jerked a thumb towards the side-piece and looked at the banker.

"Go pour me out a drink, Tuttle," he ordered.

For a moment Tuttle remained in his chair, his eyes going to Stella's face as if expecting her to countermand the order. Not by as much as a flicker of an eyelid did she show any sign of interest. Slowly and reluctantly, Tuttle went across the room and poured out a drink from the crystal decanter on the side-piece. He fetched the drink to Howkins and handed it over.

"I've told you before about drinking at this hour of the day, Harry," Stella said calmly. "Throw it into the fireplace."

Fury blazed in the slim young man's eyes, but he knew better than disobey his sister. Ever since his early childhood, Stella alone could tame his rage-filled tantrums and control him. Suddenly he hurled the glass and whisky across the room into the empty fireplace.

"You haven't got me that *sabino* yet!" he accused.

"That's right," Stella agreed. "I haven't."

"Then when are——"

It appeared to be Stella's day for interrupting people.

Raising her right hand, she pointed to the door. "Run along to your room!" she ordered. "I'm busy at the moment."

Swinging around, Howkins stormed from the room, slamming the door savagely behind him. In the hall he stood for a moment, blind rage sending shivers through his thin frame. He wanted to break something, to hear the crash of destruction. Yet to do so would bring down his sister's wrath on his head and he feared that enough to cool his other emotions. The spasm passed and a kind of primeval cunning took its place. Where Stella had a cool, incisive brain which planned well, her younger brother could only produce a kind of shrewd, sneaking cunning.

A sly grin creased Howkins' face and he ran up the stairs to his room. Knowing her brother, Stella tried to keep liquor beyond his reach, but he had managed to obtain and hide away two bottles of the best bonded whisky the Blue Bull stocked. Closing his room's door, he took the bottles from hiding, slipping them under his jacket and went to his dressing table. He opened the top drawer and rooted under the handkerchiefs and ties, taking out a set of brass knuckledusters. Slipping the evil thing over the fingers of his right hand, he looked down at the brassy glint and felt power oozing into him. With that metal sheath to his hand, he felt capable of handling anything that came along. For a moment he stood glaring into the mirror, his face bestial in its savage lust. Then he removed the knuckleduster, dropped it into his pocket, made sure the whisky bottles could not be seen, and left the room.

Going out of the rear of the house, Howkins made his way to the bunkshack. He looked into the long wooden building, finding most of the crew present. The two men he sought were lounging on their beds.

"Matic, Cheem," he said. "Let's take a ride."

None of the assembled men found anything strange in the order, being aware of the ever-present watchers and knowing the reason for the constant surveillance. According to Stella's orders, her brother was at no time allowed to leave the house's immediate area without an escort. For some reason Matic and Cheem usually found themselves elected for the task of guarding Howkins; not that they objected, for he invariably showed them a good time and it never cost them a red cent, no matter how much they drank or what they did when with him.

"What's up, boss?" asked Matic, feeding Howkins' ego by the use of the title.

"We're taking a ride, boys," Howkins replied. "Got me a couple of bottles, we'll just ride out, drink them, and think about poor old Furst."

Knowing nothing of her brother's actions, or she would have stopped them before they started, Stella settled down to work as soon as he left the room. Whenever he visited the ranch, Tuttle brought out the latest results of his and Kimble's work for Stella's inspection. He collected the books and a thick wad of money from his saddlebags and took them to the sitting-room. Then Tuttle stood back and watched the speed with which she checked his figures. As always he felt awe almost, watching the way she could total a column of figures. Good mathematician he might be, but he felt like a babe in arms compared with Stella Howkins.

Early in their association, Tuttle discovered that Stella's system of book-keeping left no loophole for the type of speculation which put him into her hands. She knew to a cent how much money came in to the bank and expected an exact accounting of it when Tuttle visited her.

"Business wasn't quite so brisk this week," Tuttle said nervously, watching her slim fingers count through the sheaf of money.

"I don't suspect you of trying to rob me," she replied. "Not because I trust your honesty, I'm not such a fool as my dear uncle, but because, unlike that business genius," the words came out bitter as bile and full of venom, "I have devised a system by which I can detect any attempt of robbing me as soon as it happens."

"It's a pity your uncle didn't have it," Tuttle answered bitterly, wondering if, after all, a spell in jail would not be preferable to his present way of life.

"I offered it to him," Stella hissed. "And he laughed, so indulgently. 'Yes, Stella, my dear, a splendid idea. Now trot off to the opera with your friends.' "

Suddenly Tuttle realized the last words had not been spoken to him. Stella sat rigid in her chair, glaring out of the window, yet not seeing the range. It was the first time he had ever seen her iron façade slip, and could guess at the force driving her on, turning her from a charming young woman into a ruthless machine with only one aim in life.

Before Tuttle could decide how he might turn his knowledge into use, Wigg entered the room.

"Bunch of cattle coming in, boss," he said.

A shudder ran through Stella's frame and for a moment she sat without looking at her foreman and top gun. Then she swung towards him and appeared to have almost regained her usual calm.

"Cattle?" she repeated, needing just a moment longer to regain full control of herself.

"Looks like Packey Pawson to me," Greenwood told her, following Wigg into the room. "He's one of the fellers I saw while I was out. Got here quicker than I expected, and brought along some fine samples just like he was a whisky drummer."

"Which way is he coming?" she asked, a thought striking her.

"From the south-west," Wigg answered.

"Let's go and meet him," ordered Stella. "Fetch my horse, Greenwood."

Packy Pawson rode to meet the approaching party, his eyes studying the two gunhands, ignoring the banker, and finally taking Stella in. Having an eye for the ladies, Packey started to mentally strip Stella, caught the cold stare she directed at him and changed his mind in a hurry. Like that blond feller on the range said, there was one gal it would not pay to monkey with. Crossing her would be more dangerous than patting the head of a stick-teased rattle-snake.

"Howdy, ma'am," he greeted. "Brought along a hundred head. All prime breeding stock, counter-branded with the Lazy H."

"Run them past me," Stella ordered.

"Sure thing, ma'am. Like I said, they're all prime critters——"

"You know my terms, so forget the sales talk!" Stella snapped.

Seeing there would be no chance of bargaining, and being aware of the danger of refusing the offer—with the Lazy H counter-branded on the cattle, Packey suddenly realized that any attempt to drive them away could be classed as cow-stealing and no court in the West would object to a rancher's men killing cow thieves—the bearded man turned and yelled an order to his trail crew. Showing considerable skill, the four riders thinned their herd into a single line and filed it by the Lazy H party.

Suddenly Stella's forefinger stabbed towards the passing line. "That black and white bull!" she snapped. "I said I wouldn't take any male animal over four years of age. That one looks at least six. Cut it out, I don't want it."

An admiring grin twisted Packey's lips. "And I figured I could get it by. Keep it as a cull, ma'am, you don't need to pay me for it."

"I've no intention of paying you for it," Stella stated flatly.

"By cracky, though, ma'am, you sure know cattle," enthused the cow thief. "That bull'd got by most folks."

"Don't try it again," she warned, but her voice showed the man's praise gave her pleasure.

On her arrival in Texas, Stella knew little or nothing about cattle. However, Wigg—one of the few hired guns with a thorough knowledge of the ranching business—taught her all he knew and, as ever, she proved an apt pupil.

"Ninety-nine head," Stella said, as the last animal

went by. "Did you see anybody on your way here?"

"No, ma'am, can't say I did," lied Packey.

"Come up to the house and I'll pay you. If you go into town to spend some of the money, watch what you say and do. I know what Greenwood told you, but at the moment there's a Ranger in town."

"A Ranger?" gulped Packey, for Greenwood had assured him that the law would not trouble any of Stella's business associates in Moondog.

"A tall, blond-haired, good-looking young man. He wears cowhand clothing and has two staghorn-butted Colts, one turned butt forward."

"But he said——!" Packey burst out.

"Who said what?" snapped Stella, as the cow thief's words died off.

"We met that feller on the range," Packey told her.

"You said you met nobody!" Stella barked.

"He told me he worked for you," Packey explained hurriedly. "Way he rode up, I never thought any different. Then he said you'd sent him to ride line, but that he was going into town to see his gal instead of doing it; and that he'd make trouble if I told you different. I didn't know he was a Ranger."

Cold fury gripped Stella and the order to kill Packey's party quivered on her lips. Then cold reason held her words. If she gave the order and word of the killing got out, other cow thieves contacted by Greenwood—and on whom she relied to rebuild her storm-decimated herds—would believe she did it to avoid paying for the cattle brought in.

"Did he ask any questions, or see the brands?" she asked.

"Just passed the time of day. I reckon he saw the brands. But Greenwood told us you'd fixed bills-of-sale to cover them."

"Don't worry, I have them. Go tell your men to push the herd on to the range and then collect your money."

"Sure, ma'am," answered a relieved Packey and galloped after his herd.

"What about Fog now?" Greenwood growled.

"He'll have to be killed," Wigg went on. "He's seen too much, just like the first pair."

"You're right," Stella agreed. "I want that Ranger dead—but not until I know whether he told Tuttle the truth about the rest of his company being at Carrintown."

"How about Packey?" Greenwood inquired. "Reckon we ought to——"

"No!" Stella answered. "We need him to prove that I keep my word about the payment, and because he can bring in more stock. When will the other men you saw be coming to see me?"

"Should be rolling in any day now," replied the ex-Ranger.

"Then we want Pawson, or whatever you called him, alive and able to tell the others that I keep my word. By the way, have either of you seen Harry?"

"Took a ride," Wigg replied. "We saw him, Matic and Cheem, on the town trail as we came to tell you about Packey's cattle. Would have gone over and fetched him back, only we figured you'd want to hear the news first."

"Any reason why you should have fetched him back?" asked Stella coldly.

"They were passing a bottle among them like it was going out of style," answered Wigg. "Harry's not the quietest feller when he's liquored up."

Normally such criticism of her brother would have brought in angry rebuke from Stella. For once none came as she realized the implication of Wigg's words. Stella knew her brother too well to place the wrong motive on his actions and cold concern bit into her.

"Wigg, Greenwood!" she snapped. "Go to Moondog and get Harry back here."

"How about——," Wigg began.

"Do what I say!" she yelled. "And just pray that you get there in time."

## CHAPTER NINE

## Here's Your Tough Ranger

While riding along Moondog's Main Street towards the livery barn, Danny saw Kimble peering through the post office's window. Ignoring the man, Danny turned the *sabino's* head towards the barn's door and continued into the building without a backward glance. Bescaby came from his office, walking forward with an expression of relief on his face. However before the man could start to tell Danny how he delayed Tuttle's arrival at the Lazy H, they heard hurrying footsteps and Kimble entered the barn.

"Howdy, Ranger," the post office's owner greeted. "Did you find them two fellers you was asking about?"

"Not yet," Danny admitted.

"Maybe they're fixing to hit another town." Kimble suggested, watching Danny lead the *sabino* into its stall.

"Maybe I just didn't look in the right places."

"That could be."

"Where'd you suggest I look?"

"North range's no good, they'd not be up there."

"Those boys always go where they oughtn't be," Danny commented. "Maybe I'd best take a *pasear* up that ways."

"They wouldn't be up there," Kimble insisted a shade too quickly. "I'd say they'd be most likely to camp near to the Kiowa reservation, so they could slip over the line if they saw anybody after them. Or be over on the east ranges. But they'd not go on the north range."

Listening to Kimble, Danny found himself wondering how Stella Howkins would react if she heard the obvious way her man tried to steer him from searching the northern ranges of the ranch. Kimble's very insistence that the men could not hide on the northern area was enough to make Danny decide that he would concentrate his efforts in that direction in future. If there had been any prospective bank robbers in the county, they would know crossing on to an Indian reservation gave them no protection against the state-wide powers of a Texas Ranger. From what he saw when surveying the country from high points, the eastern ranges offered too little cover for men wishing to hide their presence to use and hope to remain undetected.

"Reckon you know the range better than I do," Danny remarked, stripping the saddle from his *sabino*. I'll give the east range a whirl next time I'm out."

Relief flickered on to Kimble's face. "When'll that be?" he asked, then continued hurriedly, "There might be some urgent message come for you, and I'll know where to send it."

"I sure do admire a helpful town," Danny said.

"Then you'll let me know when you're going out again?" asked Kimble eagerly, seeing a chance to put one over on Tuttle.

"Why sure," promised Danny. "And let you know which way I'm going."

Kimble stayed in the barn, making small talk with Danny while the Ranger attended to his horse. At last Danny finished and, swinging his saddle on to his shoulder, he walked away from the stall. On reaching the door of the barn he turned to Kimble, who followed on his heels.

"Say, didn't you forget what you came to see Mr. Bescaby about?"

A look of surprise crossed Kimble's face and he did not reply for a long moment. Clearly he could not think of any reason for visiting the barn, and he knew better than admit that he only came to spy on Danny.

At last an inspiration came. "You haven't posted your feed order off yet, Bescaby," he said.

"I'll get round to it," Bescaby answered.

"Forget their heads some of 'em," Kimble remarked to Danny.

"They're sure lucky to have such a helpful gent at the post office," Danny replied, and looked to where the owner of the hardware store approached them.

"Can you let Miss Howkins know that dynamite she ordered's arrived?" the man asked Kimble.

Danny saw the angry glance Kimble directed at the storekeeper and wondered what the owner of the Lazy H wanted with dynamite. Of course, there could be a number of legitimate uses a working rancher found for high explosives, clearing blocked-up streams, blasting out stumps, making roads, being only a few. Yet Kimble's attitude told Danny that something deeper, more sinister, lay behind the purchase.

"I'll let her know," growled Kimble, and looked at Danny, wondering what kind of excuse he might make for his employer's purchase of dynamite.

Fortunately for Kimble, for he could think of no reason and might have even further roused the Ranger's suspicions, Danny walked away as if the words meant nothing to him. Danny had no wish to weaken his growing hold on the town by making a move which could bring injury or rebuke on to a citizen's head. There would be time enough to investigate the purpose of the purchase when he had a few friends at his back.

On reaching the hotel, Danny took his room key from Connie and could tell she wanted to speak with him. Before a word could be said, Pedro made his appearance and prevented private conversation. The girl asked if Danny enjoyed his ride, he said he had and went upstairs to his room.

Although the door was locked, Danny found that it had not stayed that way. He walked into the room and saw that the contents of his warbag lay tipped on the bed and scattered, as if somebody searched each item.

Stepping out of the room, Danny walked to the head of the stairs.

"Miss Hooper!" he called. "Can you come up here, please?"

The girl came fast, with Pedro on her heels. On entering Danny's room she stared around. Then she swung towards the Mexican, an accusation plain on her face. Danny cut in before the girl put her thoughts into words and found herself in bad trouble.

"Who's been up here?" he asked, throwing her a warning glance and hoping she read it right.

"I——," Connie began.

"Maybe it was that feller I saw when you was out this afternoon, *senorita*?" Pedro suggested blandly.

"Which feller's that?" Danny asked.

"A cowboy, *senor*. Tall, young, dressed the ordinary way. He came downstairs and walked out of the hotel. I didn't see which way he went."

"And you didn't stop him?" Connie snapped.

"No, *senorita*. I thought maybe he come in for a room while I was sleeping last night. Did he steal anything, *senor*?"

"Doesn't look that way," Danny replied.

"Couldn't we call in the town marshal?" Connie asked. "Pedro could go——"

"Reckon the marshal'd do any good, ma'am?" Danny inquired.

"He might be able to help you locate the cowboy," Connie explained.

"You know our marshal, *senorita*," grinned Pedro. "He wouldn't do any good at all."

Anger glowed in Connie's eyes when Danny appeared to agree with the Mexican. She had hoped to get rid of the Mexican so as to tell Danny of Bescaby and Weaver's spark of rebellion. However, Danny could see that the girl made her desire too obvious and that any attempt to send Pedro away would arouse the Mexican's suspicions. So Danny refused to allow Connie to place herself in a position of danger.

"Say, that cowhand wouldn't have been a feller

about my size, slim, dark, with a scar on his right cheek, and toting a matched brace of ivory-handled Army Colts?'' he asked. ''There's a feller like that goes around robbing hotel rooms.''

A crafty glint came to Pedro's face. ''*Si, senor*. You know him?''

''Reckon I do. If he's around, it'd be a sight to see.''

''He wanted ver' bad, Ranger?'' the Mexican went on.

''There's folks'd pay money to see him dead.''

Which was true enough as far as it went. Apart from the habit of robbing hotel rooms, the description fitted Captain Jules Murat, Danny's commanding officer. Danny's only intention in asking the question had been to take Connie's mind off her desire to see him and pass on news. It appeared to be working, for the girl's face changed to its usual calm lines. Suddenly she realized what Danny saw from the start and knew she must not make that mistake again.

''I can't tell you how sorry I am about this, Ranger,'' she stated. ''If you find anything missing, let me know and I'll make it good to you.''

''Thanks ma'am,'' Danny replied, going through his property swiftly. ''It's all there.''

''Then I'll go down and arrange for a meal for you, and Pedro can get back to his work.''

''Sure, ma'am,'' Danny agreed. ''Sorry to have taken up your time.''

After Connie and Pedro left the room, Danny turned his attention to the bed once more. He knew, or could guess at, the reason for the search. Pedro hoped to find a list of the code words which would keep the Rangers in Carrintown informed of Danny's continued well-being. In a way, the search relieved Danny's feelings a little. Clearly Stella Howkins had not yet managed to break his bluff, or she would never have ordered the search.

For all that, Danny knew he worked on a razor's edge and one slip would mean death. At any moment the owner of the Lazy H might learn that his apparent pat-hand contained nothing more than a low card bluff.

Maybe the cow thief, Packey, would let slip out word of their meeting; or might even remember where he last saw Danny, which would bring an instant warning to Stella Howkins. In either case, Danny's position grew more precarious. Once she learned that no Ranger force awaited his signal to Carrintown, Danny knew his life-expectancy would be counted in hours.

Maybe the prudent thing would be to pull out, make a fast ride to the county seat and telegraph Murat for help. But Danny knew he could not take the obvious, and safe, course. His instincts told him that he had stirred up a tiny spark of rebellion among the citizens of Moondog. If he ran out and left them, their resistance would collapse and never rise again, no matter how many men he brought back with him.

So Danny knew he must make it a case of root, hog, or die, and stand his ground, taking his chances in the hope that he could hold out until Murat arrived. If Murat came too late—well, Danny tried not to let *that* thought worry him. One thing he must do was leave word of his findings. Somehow he must make sure that the Rangers who came after him, should they arrive too late, had a good start in the business of breaking Stella Howkins' reign of terror.

A smarter man than Pedro would have taken pencil and notebook from Danny's belongings, fortunately the Mexican had not thought to take such a precaution against Danny leaving evidence behind him. From the dirty thumb-mark on one page Danny concluded the Mexican had looked through the book, but, finding nothing in it to interest him, left it and the pencil behind.

After repacking most of his belongings in the warbag, Danny sat on the bed and took up the writing materials. Carefully he started to write a detailed report of everything that had happened to him since his arrival. He put down what he knew of conditions in the town, adding all Connie told him on her secret visit, without mentioning the source of his information. From there he covered his search of the range, the meeting of the cow thieves, drawing his own conclusions of Stella's motives. He stated that he believed she supported her hired guns at the expense of the people they terrorized, but could offer no reason for why she needed the small army of hired fighting men. Taking his time, thinking out every word, he forgot nothing. Packey's mention of Stella's offer to pay bounty on every Kiowa killed went to the paper, as did Danny's hearing about the consignment of dynamite for the Lazy H. When at last he had finished the report, a full account of his actions and findings lay in cold print.

Once the report was finished, Danny gave thought to keeping it safe until the arrival of the reinforcements. If something went wrong, he wanted to ensure his work would not be in vain. So he could not keep the book on his person, nor in his warbag. If he knew Stella Howkins, should anything happen to him she would insist on a very thorough search being made for anything that might lead his fellow Rangers to her.

Looking around the room, Danny saw no safe hiding place. Then he remembered his brother Dusty's advice on such matters. Instead of placing the book in some well-concealed spot—where thorough searchers would be sure to locate it—he went to the window. Outside, night had fallen and the room he occupied could not be overlooked from any of the surrounding buildings. Carefully, he raised the sash and looked out at the balcony which ran along before the rooms. Access to this could only be made by climbing through the window, due to a mistake in the building of the hotel, and the balcony was little used. Danny leaned forward to make sure that nobody watched him from the other rooms, then tossed the notebook along to fall by the balcony rail and in front of the next room's window. With that done, he closed his room's window and secured it.

"Reckon that ought to hold it," he thought. "I sure hope that I never need that book though."

If he did not, it would be because he remained alive and gave his report verbally to Captain Murat.

With the report attended to, Danny packed away the pencil. Then he slung on his gunbelt, tied down the holsters and checked the Colts. Putting on his hat, he left the room and walked downstairs. He entered the dining-room and went to a table. There had been no stage-coach in that day and he was the only roomer. Connie came to the table, fussing around it and keeping her back to where Pedro stood at the door.

Also with his back to the Mexican, Danny spoke to the girl, keeping his voice down low.

"I've written a report and hid it," he said. "Don't you worry none, there's nothing in it to bring them down on you."

"I can rely on you for that," the girl answered and went on in a louder voice, "I've been holding a meal for you, Mr. Fog. I hope it will be all right."

"Reckon it will, ma'am," Danny replied in his normal voice. "If it's not, then I'm to blame, I fell asleep up there."

Pedro had been concerned about Danny's non-arrival, but the words calmed his suspicions.

Although the meal had been warmed up a second time, it went down well. Danny made no attempt to communicate further with the girl and she disappeared after serving him. With his meal finished, Danny rose and walked from the hotel. Outside, he stood for a moment looking around him. Down at the saloon a piano tinkled, but it sounded as out-of-place as hearty laughter at a funeral.

While walking along the street, Danny decided his best plan would be to go to the saloon first. If Tuttle, Kimber or Drager suggested that he sent off his message to Carrintown, he could assume that his bluff still held good. Should the men not remind him of his 'duty'— well, he would meet that situation when it arrived.

The attack came suddenly, viciously, and completely unexpectedly.

Alert though he was, Danny's senses reacted just a shade too slowly to his danger. Even as he passed the corner of the building preceding the saloon, he saw two shapes moving out of the blackness of the alley. His attention was on them, his brain sending orders for defence, when something smashed into the side of his face. The blow came from the corner he was just passing. Taken by itself, the attack lacked power; but the hand that struck Danny had a brass knuckle-duster to supplement its power.

Sharp and unexpected though the pain of the blow had been, it did not have the power to put Danny out of action for long. Given a couple of seconds, he could have handled the attacker. Only he was not granted that long. Springing forward, one of the two shapes lashed up a foot. His boot drove into Danny's groin. Pure undistilled, soul-tearing agony knifed through Danny, doubling him over and sending him sprawling into the hitching rail. The slim shape that launched the first blow darted forward and crashed another punch at the side of Danny's head. Then he was shoved aside so that his two companions could make a more scientific and effective attack.

"Get him!" the slim shape screeched hysterically. "Stomp him!"

Through the pain which filled him, Danny recognized Howkins' voice. Only, by that time he was too far gone to make anything of his information. Three raging, cursing, shapes swarmed around him; feet and fists thudded him. For what seemed like an age Danny's body went through purgatory, then blackness and lack of feeling welled over it. Even though the limp body went to the sidewalk, the three attackers made no attempt to slow their assault.

Attracted by the noise, men burst from the saloon and stared to where the three shapes mauled the still form on the ground. Every man present guessed what was happening. A low growl left Bescaby's lips and his hands clenched. Then he felt somebody grip his bicep and swung around to face Doctor Drager.

"Your wife's still sick, Bescaby," the man warned.

"Get back inside all of you!" Kimble ordered an instant later. "You hear me. Get back in there!"

The fear inspired by Stella Howkins' men brought obedience. Last to go was Bescaby. Fury welled in him and he wanted to rush along the sidewalk in a rescue attempt. Then he thought of his ailing wife, a delicate woman who frequently needed medical attention. Black despair welled over him and he knew he could do nothing without endangering her life. Giving a half-strangled moan, he turned and stumbled blindly back into the saloon. Behind him the thudding impact of kicks and the raving of the three attackers continued.

Not a sound came from the saloon during the minutes that the noise of the attack continued. Every eye stayed riveted upon the batwing doors. At last Matic and Cheem appeared, walking side-by-side and following a wild-eyed flush-faced Harry Howkins. The slim young man threw open the doors and his companions dragged in the bloody, limp shape of Danny Fog.

"There's your tough Ranger!" Howkins screeched as the other two threw their burden down. "There's the feller who was going to push me and my sister——"

Hooves thundered on the street, came to a halt, and two men entered the bar.

"You damned crazy fool!" Wigg spat out, staring at Howkins, then down to the unmoving shape on the floor. "Get the hell out of here."

"You can't talk to me like that!" Howkins howled, holding up Danny's gunbelt—which he now wore insecurely about his middle—and glaring at the gunhand.

"Go pick up that *sabino* you've been wanting," Wigg answered knowing that Stella would not allow even her top gun to knock sense into her brother.

The argument worked. "Sure, Wigg," Howkins agreed. "I'll tend to that for sure. Say, we took care of him good, didn't we?"

"That you did," agreed Wigg and looked to where Drager knelt by the still form. "How bad is it, Doc?"

A scared face lifted to Wigg, for Drager realized the seriousness of the situation.

"He's—he's dead."

"So?" snarled Howkins "That's what——"

"Go collect that hoss!" Wigg snarled.

Something in the man's voice and attitude warned Howkins not to argue. In which, probably for the first time in his life, he showed real good sense. Wigg had reached the point where he no longer cared what Stella Howkins ruled about the welfare of her brother. With his neck feeling the hairy touch of a manila rope, Wigg would have knocked Howkins through the door if the other refused or argued about leaving. Turning, Howkins scuttled through the door. Suddenly cold sober and realizing what they had done, Cheem and Matic exchanged scared glances.

"You pair go with him," Wigg growled. "And stay with him. If you run, I'll have you found and killed by inches."

"Sure, Wigg," Cheem replied and left on Howkins' heels.

With the three culprits gone, Wigg turned and looked around the room. "Now listen good to me, all of you," he said. "This never happened. The Ranger never came here. No matter who comes asking, you never saw him, you know nothing. Any of you who thinks different, take a look at your family when you leave here— because we'll not leave wife or child alive should any man talk."

## CHAPTER TEN

## He's Taken His Life In His Hands

The tall, slim, dark-haired man in the cowhand clothing, waded into the mud and slipped his rope's loop
around the horns of the trapped cow. Backing off to
where his horse stood, he checked that the double
cinches and latigo straps were drawn as tight as possible,
then swung into the saddle. A streak of mud ran across
his face and the small scar on the right cheek added
rather than detracted for the handsome features. For all
that he wore mud-stained, ordinary range clothing, he
seemed to be clad in a cloak and plumed hussar uni-
form, for there was a gasconading air about him.

Mounting the horse, he allowed it to move forward
slowly until the rope grew taut. Slowly the cow came
clear, being dragged out of the mud and on to firm
ground. Dropping from his saddle, the man returned to
the cow and tailed it up, gripping the roof of its tail to
assist its rise. As soon as he completed the kindly action,
the man jumped clear and jerked off his rope, then
raced for his horse. With typical gratitude, the cow
charged its rescuer. Making a leap-frog mount, he went
over the rump of his horse and it, as used to the
behaviour of cattle at such times as was its rider, lunged
forward. The cow swung by, hooking its long horns
viciously and scraping mud from the rider's leg in
passing, then it lurched away, heading for the open
range as fast as it could go.

Captain Jules Murat was enjoying his first vacation in
four years.

Bog riding, hauling cattle out of mud-holes—they got the habit of using the area for wallowing in dry periods and failed to see the danger brought by heavy rains—being strenuous and dangerous work, the hands assigned to the task operated in pairs.

The man partnering Murat bore quite a name in Texas. At seventeen he rode as captain in command of Company 'C', the Texas Light Cavalry, and won a name for being one of the South's three best military raiders. When only barely nineteen, he went into Mexico on a mission of great importance to the uneasy peace of the United States.* He tamed a wild-wide-open town after three men died in the attempt.† Men spoke of him as segundo of the biggest ranch in Texas, a trail boss second to none, and the fastest, most accurate handler of a brace of Colts in the West.

Yet he did not look the part such a giant among his fellows should.

Dusty Fog stood at most five-foot-six and gave the impression of being even smaller—unless one saw him in time of trouble. Yet he was not puny. In fact, although few noticed it, he had the build of a miniature Hercules. He wore good clothing, yet did not set them off well, making them look like nothing. In times of peace his matched, bone-handled Army Colts rode butt forward in the cross-draw holsters of his gunbelt without drawing attention to the wearer. That belt had been made by the finest leather-worker of them all. Joe Gaylin would sell his boots, saddles, bridles or harness to anybody who met his high prices, but he only made gunbelts for men he selected to receive the honour. Dusty Fog had been one of the first to receive a Gaylin belt. One way or another, that small, dusty blond haired, handsome man from the Rio Hondo was a legend in his own right.

"That's the last one, thank the Lord," drawled Murat. "I thought you asked me down here to hunt

* Told in THE YSABEL KID
† Told in QUIET TOWN

cougar and listen to hounds making music, not to haul cows out of the mud.''

"You shouldn't've told Stanton Howard about it when he was entertaining a bunch of Eastern politicians," Dusty countered.

Murat nodded in solemn agreement. On hearing that the Rio Hondo country had a cougar smart enough to stay clear of the OD Connected's pack of hard-driving blue-tick cathounds, the Governor of Texas accepted a standing invitation to visit his friend Ole Devil Hardin. How much the Governor's decision had been influenced by his being forced to act as host to a bunch of Eastern politicians on a tour of the West had not been mentioned, but both Dusty and Murat thought that Howard's visit stemmed from that.

On the second day of the visit—a cougar-hunt, organized for visiting friends, could not be rushed into—word reached the spread of a bunch of cattle grazing by the Hickok mud hole. Most of the ranch's crew were busy on other chores about the vast area of the spread, so Dusty and Murat ignored their social position to ride out and perform the back-breaking task of rescuing the animals from their bovine stupidity.

"That was me and my big mou——," began Murat and stopped as something attracted his attention. "We've got company."

Following the direction of the other's stare, Dusty saw a youngster afork a fast-running horse approaching them.

"Cousin Vic," he remarked.

"Is there anybody lives in Rio Hondo country who isn't a Fog, Hardin or Blaze?" inquired Murat with a grin.

"Couple of folks. We're working on moving them out," smiled Dusty. "His pappy runs the Wells Fargo office. Wonder what's wrong."

Much to Dusty's surprise, the youngster brought his horse to a halt at Murat's side and held out an envelope to the Ranger captain.

"For you, Cap'n Murat," he said, then looked

towards Dusty. "Pappy sent me with it, Cousin Dusty.
Met Cousin Red on the way to the big house and he told
me where you were. I came right here."

That figured. Most of the Rio Hondo boys knew their
way around the OD Connected's ranges.

"Smart thinking, *amigo*." Dusty replied, glancing at
Murat.

"Hell fire!" the Ranger spat out after reading the
note.

"Bad news?" asked Dusty.

"It's from Danny. He's telegraphed that word came
from Moondog about me not sending the Ranger help
the folks asked for—only I sent it, two good men."

"And?" Dusty said, knowing the other would not be
so disturbed if that was all the message contained.

"He's gone up there alone to start looking for the
others." Murat answered. "I'll tell you about it on the
way to the house."

"Let's go then," Dusty replied. "How about you,
Vic?"

"Pappy wants me back at the office. See you, Cousin
Dusty."

Whirling his horse, Vic headed off in the direction he
came. Dusty and Murat pointed their mounts towards
the OD Connected's main house and let the animals
make good time.

"I'd heard rumors about Moondog," Murat explained as they rode. "Nothing certain, but enough to
make me wonder. It could've been townfolk riled at the
cowhands, or bad trouble. Only I couldn't spare the
men on rumours. Couple of times over the past year my
men've rode through and seen nothing, or heard no
complaints. Then an anonymous letter reached me."

"Must have been something to make you send men to
check it out," Dusty commented.

"I figured it was. Sent along Pinky Pugh and Mick
Salmon."

"Know them. They're smart boys."

"Sure. I didn't expect to hear from them for at least
two weeks, even if it took them that long to untangle the

trouble up there. Then Stanton insisted I took my furlough. I left Danny in charge and came over here. Now he's sent me a message that another letter arrived from Moondog, that one claims Pinky and Mick haven't got there.''

"They wouldn't tell folks they were Rangers," Dusty pointed out.

"No. But if they hadn't made their presence felt by now, things would've been tough enough for them to get word out for help. Danny's gone off alone. He's taken his life in his hands, Dusty.''

"Danny's a smart Ranger," Dusty answered.

"A damned smart Ranger," agreed Murat. "But he's only one man. I'm going up there——"

"If you think it's that serious," Dusty interrupted, "you'd best let me handle Moondog. I'll take Mark and Lon with me. We'll leave tonight. That way you can go straight to your headquarters and start gathering some of your company to back us if we need it.''

Taking all into consideration, Murat admitted Dusty suggested the best plan. That way help would be on its way to Moondog in powerful numbers. Only three men, true, but each one a top-grade fighting man to be reckoned with.

The girl's engagement ring glinted in the light of the stable's lamp as she slid her arm around the tall man's neck and snuggled to his body, kissing him in a fervour of passion. Not that any woman would have blamed her at that. Full six foot three the man stood, with tremendously broad shoulders that tapered down to a slim waist and long, powerful legs. His golden blond hair had a natural curl, and his tanned, intelligent face was almost classically handsome. Through the material of his expensive shirt, she felt hard muscles and his giant biceps squeezing her gently, sending shivers of anticipation through her.

While kissing the blond giant, she compared him with her fiance; not to the latter's advantage. Although she acknowledged that her fiance was one of the rising members of the Radical side of the Republican Party, she admitted he sadly lacked as a lover.

From what she had witnessed so far, Mark Counter had no limitations in that line.* It mattered little to her that Mark had once been the Beau Brummel of the Confederate Cavalry and now dictated dress fashions amongst the Texas cowhands. She was aware of his strength, without realizing its full potential, but many folks claimed Mark was the strongest man in the West. Not having seen him in action, she knew little of his prowess in a bar-room brawl. Nor did she know that he could claim to be better with cattle than his friend, Dusty Fog. Living in the shadow of the Rio Hondo gun wizard, Mark's gun ability received little acclaim, but men who knew put him second to Dusty in speed and accuracy.

The girl knew none of that. All she knew was that Mark Counter could sure hand out a kind of love-making which made her quiver, think of wedding bells—or at least of the wedding bed.

"Mark?" Dusty's voice came from the door. "We're pulling out in an hour."

Knowing Dusty would never interrupt him at such a tender moment unless the matter be urgent, Mark released the girl. Deprived of his support, she sat down hard and stared her disbelief as he walked towards the door.

"Mark!" she squealed. "You never showed me the golden horseshoe nail."

"You'd best ask your fiance to show you it, honey," Mark replied and left the stable.

The girl let out a furious squeak and her feet drummed on the floor in a frenzy of fury and frustration.

"Golden horseshoe nail," Dusty grunted, as he walked with Mark towards the house. "Shame on you, and her a guest, too."

"Landsakes, Dusty," Mark answered. "It was self-defence. She'd been almost sitting on my lap, filling me

---

* Also proved in TROUBLED RANGE & THE WILDCATS.

gut-deep with social-conscience and rights of the individual. I figured to bore her as much as she'd bored me.''

"I bet you did," grinned Dusty. "Where's Lon?"

"Playing billiards with her fiance. Feller got to asking me how I felt about being exploited by the cattle barons, which's when Lon got him away from me."

"Why didn't you tell Gunby about your pappy and Aunt Mathilda?" asked Dusty.

Mark's father owned a ranch not much smaller than the OD Connected and his departed Aunt Mathilda left him all her considerable fortune in her will. Taken one way and another, Mark was not suitable material for a Radical Republican to try preaching political theories on.

"Thought of it," Mark admitted. "What's wrong, Dusty?"

"Danny's in bad trouble," Dusty replied. "We'll get riding as soon as we're packed."

Even though Mark looked forward to a pleasant vacation, and despite night having fallen, the blond giant never thought to question Dusty's orders. Riding as a member of Ole Devil's floating outfit had accustomed Mark to sudden departures; and the matter sounded urgent. Mostly Dusty allowed his younger brother to stand on his own capable two feet. If the small Texan felt the situation warranted going to Danny's aid, Mark would not raise objections.

"I'll get Lon, you see Ole Devil," he suggested as they entered the house.

Both players in the billiard game had a problem. While being a stout supporter of the rights of the individual, provided those rights coincided with his political views, and a defender of the working man against exploitation by the employers, Gavin Gunby wondered if he should win the game and pocket the wagered thirty dollars, or allow his opponent to snatch a narrow victory as a lure to making a bigger bet. He soothed his political conscience with the thought that the other player was too young to vote and would probably support the Democrats when old enough, and also had such privileges that he must be a boss's man, so as such could be bilked in an attempt to show him the error of his ways.

"Tight game," he remarked, after taking a no-scoring shot that left the balls scattered around the table.

"Real tight," agreed the Ysabel Kid, studying the situation and chalking his cue solemnly.

"Only seven in it," Gunby went on, failing to mention that he needed to score only two more points to make a hundred and give him the game.

"Yep, I reckon I'll do it this time."

Studying the table, Gunby knew he could not make a score from the balls in their present position, so, of course, no lesser person would be able to do so.

"We could go another five dollars on it" suggested the guardian against exploitation.

"Make it ten," answered the exploited, "poor lil half-smart Texas boy like me can't count real well in fives."

For a moment suspicion filled Gunby as he studied the lean figure before him. Taking in the handsome, almost babyishly-innocent, Indian-dark face, the curly, deep black hair, the black clothing, Gunby made a mistake.

Not that he was the first man to fail to see the Ysabel Kid's full potential until too late.

Born of a wild Irish-Kentuckian father and a French-Creole Comanche mother, the Kid drew something from each of his bloods. From his father came a tough independence and the sighting eye of an eagle when using a rifle. His mother's Comanche strain passed on the ability to ride anything with four legs and hair, skill in following tracks, super prowess at riding scout and silent movement. Always a nation of steel-users, the French-Creole blood gave the Kid a love for the razor-edged James Black bowie knife as a fighting weapon. The knife and his Winchester Model '66 rifle formed his first loves in time of war, but it must be admitted that at such moments his belt also supported a walnut-handled old colt Dragoon revolver, butt forward at the right side. Of course, he could not claim to be *real* fast with a gun, but he had proved himself to be no mean performer when using it. Fast, deadly as any Indian—about whom he knew much—the Kid made a good friend and a bad enemy.

Gunby knew none of that. All he saw being a slim, young-looking cowhand who imagined he could play billiards. Only by playing down to the Kid had Gunby managed to raise the betting to thirty dollars. After another look at the table, Gunby gave a nod of agreement.

"Forty it is," he said.

At which point Mark Counter looked into the billiard room and said, "Lon, we're pulling out in an hour."

The words solved the Kid's problem.

"Be right there," he said, and bent over the table.

Erecting his bridge with the fingers of the left hand, the Kid rested his cue on it and took careful sight. Twice he worked the cue back and forwards then he stabbed the ball. With bugged-out eyes, Gunby watched the ball race along the table to clip his ball into the centre pocket. From there the Kid's ball screwed itself in a spinning line, hit the red for a cannon and deposited it in the top right-hand pocket. After that the white ball struck three cushions and flopped obediently into the lower left-hand pocket.

"Landsakes," said the Kid. "They all went in. That's ten points, they do tell me."

"Wh—I——You——!" spluttered Gunby.

"Old Comanche saying," drawled the Kid, holding out his left hand palm upwards. "Keep bow strung, sharp edge on war lance, always collect gambling debts straight away. Forty dollars, wasn't it?"

The Kid's problem had been exactly the same as Gunby's, should he take the money or lay back in the hope of a larger bet on the next game. Although Gunby had not known the fact, the Kid played billiards with the same precision that he handled a rifle.

"I'm sorry to spoil you pair's fun," Dusty told his friends.

"I'm not," Mark answered. "That sure was a demanding woman."

"Anyways," the Kid went on as they walked upstairs to their rooms. "You told us to entertain the guests."

"I said entertain them, not——," began Dusty.

"That's what we were doing," Mark objected. "Lon entertained Gunby and I stopped his gal from getting bored."

"Fine examples of Southern hospitality!" Dusty grunted.

"Is Danny in a bad tight?" Mark asked, as they prepared to go to their rooms.

"Could be real bad," agreed Dusty. "I hope we get to him before anything happens."

## CHAPTER ELEVEN

## I Feel I've Known You All My Life

Whenever the cares of running the Lazy H grew too much for her to bear, Stella Howkins liked to ride alone and found doing so relaxed her. She felt the need of relaxation on the morning after Danny Fog's death. From the moment her brother returned to the house, full of himself at having removed the menace Danny offered to her plans, Stella had been busy. Wigg brought Danny's body to the ranch and arranged for it to be taken and buried alongside the first pair of Rangers. Having chosen the spot herself, Stella doubted if anything but the most thorough and painstaking search would locate the graves. There had been other details to handle. Stella guessed that Danny Fog left a report of his findings and sent Wigg to make a search for it. Although the gunhand almost took Danny's room apart and went through the Ranger's property item by item, he found nothing. Nor could Stella do better when Wigg delivered Danny's property to her. Pedro, summoned from the hotel, claimed that at no time had the Ranger and Connie Hooper been in a position to converse in private or to change possession of any papers. Stella finally decided she might be wrong about the existence of the report.

Although Wigg wanted to send men into town, Stella refused. She knew the people of Moondog and felt sure that waiting for her men to come would have a far more chilling effect than the presence of hired guns. Tuttle, Kimble and Drager were capable of watching the town

119

and Pedro kept a fast horse ready to bring word should extra help be needed. There was another reason why Stella wanted her men on hand. That morning the heads of two cow thief gangs arrived to see her and brought news that three more of their kind would arrive later in the day. Stella wanted to impress her visitors with her ranch's armed strength and give them a gentle warning of what to expect if they tried to double-cross her. So she ignored the town, knowing that the death of the Ranger would have a salutary effect on its citizens. Even those who might have taken heart at Danny Fog's handling of her men would now be back to their old state of submissive terror again.

Stella's horse came to a sudden halt, throwing back its head and snorting. Jolted from her thoughts, she looked around for the cause of the animal's actions. The horse stood on the top of a slope and at its foot, sprawled stiff in death, lay a bull. Giving an angry tongue-cluck, Stella nudged her horse's ribs and wondered at the animal's refusal to move forward. Normally the horse, her favourite mount, obeyed her orders, yet for some reason, it seemed reluctant to go down the slope into the valley. At last she managed to coax the horse to the foot of the slope, but it refused to advance. Slipping from the saddle, Stella tied the reins to a nearby bush and advanced towards the dead bull on foot.

Even as she walked forward, Stella became aware that all was not well. Some living creature killed the bull and fed on its flesh, that showed plainly. An instant later Stella learned the identity of the killer. She heard a rustling in the bushes some yards from where she stood, then a hideous snarling roar rose into the air. Behind her, the horse screamed and reared high in terror, tore free its reins and bolted blindly away. With it went Stella's only means of defence, for the quirt, hanging by its thong from her wrist was of no use against a grizzly bear bent on protecting its kill. Stella always carried a Winchester carbine on her saddle when riding the range, but it was more for the purpose of signalling or hunting than as a weapon. The unseen watchers of her house never troubled her, even though she never took an escort when on one of her relaxation-inducing rides. To that day she never found any need of a weapon.

For the first time in her life Stella realized just what raw, animal-blind fear meant. Never had she felt so completely inadequate and unable to cope with a situation than at that moment. The fear bit down into her, driving any hope of cohesive thought from her head. Death, savage, primeval and terrifying, stared her in the face. Her legs buckled under her and she sank to her knees. Much as she wanted to close her eyes, she could not, and so continued to stare at the huge, shaggy shape that advanced with terrible purpose towards her. Just one scream burst from her throat; the soul-wrenching cry of a woman in mortal peril.

Only one thing saved Stella from instant death. On sinking to her knees, she froze in terror and the bear did not charge as it would if she made a move. Slowly it came nearer, rising on its hind legs, huge and terrible, standing swaying with an arched forward neck. Stella stayed rigid, her eyes locked on the bear's huge-fanged jaws, the raw beast smell of it clogging her nostrils. In a moment she would move and on that movement bring about a charge.

On the opposite slope of the valley hooves thundered and Dusty Fog sent the big *bayo-coyote* gelding he sat, racing forward. Leaning down, he jerked the Winchester carbine from the saddleboot.

While coming unnoticed by Stella on the other side of the valley, Dusty saw her approaching the dead bull and opened his mouth in a warning. He figured her to be a dude. No Western-born woman would have gone near such an object as the bull, at least, not without real good cause and being in possession of a rifle. Before Dusty could shout, the bear made its appearance. A grizzly bear would always lie up and sleep close to its kill, ready to protect it from intruders.

For once Dusty found himself wishing he carried a heavier calibre weapon than his Winchester Model '66 carbine, for he admitted that the little saddle-gun left much to be desired under the circumstances. While ideal for its purpose, being light, compact, easily handled, and with a twelve-shot magazine that purpose had never been hunting grizzly bears—especially under the conditions facing Dusty at that moment.

Nor did the horse between his knees make matters any easier. The big paint stallion that crippled Dusty's uncle, Ole Devil,* and which Dusty now used as his personal mount, had thrown a shoe and picked up a stone bruise during the fast ride from the OD Connected. Fortunately, a friend's ranch lay close at hand and there Dusty left his horse, knowing it would be well cared for. He also took the pick of his friend's spare horses. The detour led him out of his way, so he let Mark and the Kid continue following the winding stage-coach route to Moondog. On collecting the *bayo-coyote* gelding from his friend, he cut across country in a direct line towards the town. While the horse ate work and had been well-trained, it showed a marked reluctance to riding down on a grizzly bear.

Knowing he would need to shoot fast and straight; and that he could not do so from the fiddle-footing horse; Dusty unshipped from the saddle. He lit down running, while the horse swung away from him, then halted under the feel of its trailing reins.

Even as he ran, Dusty knew he must act fast. Only the girl's immobility had saved her so far, but that might end at any moment. A yell left Dusty's lips, bringing the bear's head swinging towards him. Seeing a moving shape, the bear turned its fury in that direction. Nor did Dusty's first bullet make the bear less aggressively inclined. Taken on the run, the bullet ripped into the bear's side and inflicted a painful wound.

Stella heard the yell and shot, turning her eyes towards the sound. Through the fear burst realization that a saviour had arrived. She saw the bear chage at Dusty, heard the rapid cracking of the carbine as he blurred off

* Told in THE FASTEST GUN IN TEXAS

shot after shot at the rushing animal.

After throwing five shots into the bear, Dusty still failed to put it down. On it rushed, snarling and bristling in awesome rage. Dusty forced himself to take careful aim, sighting down and knowing just how little time he had to send home a bullet that would save his life. An inch to the right or left and, before he could work the lever to feed another round into the gun's chamber, the bear would be on him. After that it would be all over bar the snarling.

The carbine cracked and its flat-nosed .44 Henry bullet slammed between the bear's eyes. Staggering, the huge animal started to go down and Dusty threw himself to one side. He was only just in time, the bear's huge body brushed against him as it crashed to the ground. Working another round into the carbine, Dusty swung to face the bear, but found his further attention unnecessary.

Lowering the carbine, Dusty raised a hand and wiped the sweat from his face. He figured a man could spend two lifetimes without wanting to go through such an experience again. While a keen hunter, Dusty still had no wish to tangle with another fully-grown grizzly bear unless carrying a more suitable weapon.

After a couple of seconds necessary to shake off the effect of as narrow an escape as ever came his way, Dusty turned and walked towards the girl he saved from death. Stella rose, face ashy pale, body shaking with hysteria and beyond her control. Walking forward, Dusty saw that gentle methods would be a waste of time. He swung his left hand, its palm catching the girl's cheek hard enough to sting through the hysteria. Next moment Stella collapsed into his arms, sobbing and clinging to him. For the first time in her life, she wanted to be protected, to have the strong arms of a man around her, shielding her from danger.

Gently, Dusty led the girl past the bear's body. As she drew near to the great, still twitching shape, she instinctively drew closer to Dusty and his arms supported her. At the side of the *bayo-coyote*, he thrust away the carbine. Stella looked back at the bear's body and shuddered.

"Take me away from it!" she moaned.

Still supporting the girl, Dusty led her to the slope and behind a clump of bushes. Once out of sight of the bear, he lowered her into a sitting position on the ground. Suddenly, she twisted towards him, locking her arms around his neck, drawing him down beside her, mouth reaching hungrily, passionately towards his.

All Stella's held-down passions, a woman's inborn desire to love and be loved, welled forth as a reaction to her narrow escape from death. Savagely she kissed Dusty and his arms went about her as he kissed back. In that moment there was no resisting the primeval call. Even had he known Stella's identity and about his brother's death, Dusty could not have held himself back from returning her kisses. Like Stella, he had been under severe emotional strain and the reaction affected him in much the same manner; although he would probably have recovered from it quickly enough had she not been present.

"Love me!" Stella moaned, clinging to him and kissing him again. "Please love me!"

Almost an hour later Dusty mounted the *bayo-coyote* gelding and swung the girl up before him on to the saddle. Instantly she snuggled as close as possible to him, mouth open and tongue tip showing as she tried to reach his lips again. All Stella's years of loveless devotion to achieving her goal in life were forgotten. Never had she felt such an emotion as while locked in Dusty's arms and fulfilling a woman's functions. The reaction to her narrow escape wore off during their love-making, but Stella felt different; just how different she did not realize.

Once the first pangs of reaction died off, Stella studied her rescuer. She saw beyond the unshaven, trail-dirty, five-foot-six of human frame to the real, big powerful man that was Dusty Fog. Instinctively she knew that she had found the one man who could master her; the one man worthy of the love and devotion she knew herself capable of giving. So she yielded herself to him, not out of the primeval reaction of being saved from death, but freely and without restraint and with all her heart behind each caress.

"Where now?" asked Dusty, holding her away.

"Wherever you want to go," she sighed.

"You'd best make the choice," he countered.

"Take me to my house."

"And where'd that be?"

"Go across the valley and make for that hill with the clump of trees on its peak. You'll see the place from there."

"Just hold on then," Dusty drawled.

"I will!" she breathed, then a thought struck her. "We don't know each other's names. I'm Stella Howkins. What can I call you?"

Dusty had guessed the girl's identity once the fog of reaction had left him, drawing his conclusions from her expensive clothing and the knowledge that he rode on the Lazy H's land. However, he did not want her to learn his true identity.

"Edward Marsden," he told her.

Which in itself was not a lie. Dusty had been christened Dustine Edward Marsden Fog.

Now the primeval reaction to rising triumphant from a conflict with a large and dangerous animal had died away, Dusty could think rationally once again. This was the woman who, if Murat's information be true, ruled a town with terror and hired guns. It might be best to prevent her learning his name, in case she knew his brother Danny's conection with the Rangers. Dusty knew he could learn plenty from Stella, but not if she discovered his true identity.

"I want you to stay at the house with me, Edward," she told him, still holding tight to his torso and with her face pressed against his.

"We've only just met," Dusty pointed out.

"I feel I've known you all my life," she answered, then a hint of panic came into her voice, "You won't leave me, will you, Edward?"

"Look, Stella—," Dusty began.

"I'll make you happy. I'll give you anything you want. I love you, Edward, I love you!"

At that moment they saw her horse ahead of them. After fleeing, the horse ran until its panic subsided and its training to stand when the reins hung free brought it to a halt.

"Reckon we'd best go get it," Dusty remarked, not sorry to find an excuse to escape from the girl's arms.

"I'm happy enough riding like this," she answered, nuzzling his cheek with her nose and lips.

"Likely," Dusty replied, bringing the *bayo-coyote* to a halt and trying to lower the girl from the saddle. "But this horse of mine's ridden too hard to carry double much further."

"Don't bother about your horse," she cooed, clinging on to him all the harder. "I'll give you the pick of the Lazy H remuda."

A vague memory stirred in Stella as she said the last words. For a moment the cool business section of her brain tried to remind her of the last time she offered a man the pick of the Lazy H remuda. The warning failed to get through. At that moment Stella was woman pure and simple, wanting only to hold on to the man who saved her life and loved her on the slope. So, while her brain tried to tie up some nagging doubts, the rest of her resisted thinking of such unpleasant things as who her rescuer reminded her of. All she could see was that *big* man springing to her rescue, drawing the bear from her and saving her life, then treating her as no other man ever did.

Feeling the girl's arm clutching him, Dusty suddenly wanted to make an end to the affair. After those minutes on the slope, he had recovered himself and wanted only to place the girl in safety and ride away. With an almost angry gesture, he swung Stella to the ground and shook her hands from him.

"Edward!" she wailed.

"Wait here while I catch your horse!" he snapped back and swung the *bayo-coyote* gelding away from her.

Listening to the cold, clipped tones, Stella felt a shiver of delightful submission run through her. Never had any man dared to address her in such a manner and she, in her present mood, enjoyed the novel change. She wondered what he would do to her if she disobeyed, and a pleasant tingle of anticipation ran over her as she conjectured on what might happen. Possibly he would beat her; the thought did not frighten her. Once they reached the ranch, she would try disobeying him and looked forward eagerly to being taught who was master.

Collecting Stella's horse, Dusty rode back to her leading the animal. He expected an explosion, for his instincts told him that Stella was not used to taking orders, but he decided to force the issue.

"Mount up and let's ride," he ordered.

Meekly she obeyed him, still tingling to the thrill of submitting to his commands. Once astride her horse, she rode as close as possible to the gelding and reached out a hand towards Dusty. He ignored her hand, starting his horse moving with her at his side.

"I own everything as far as you can see, Edward," she told him. "It will——"

"It's good range, Stella," Dusty interrupted. "Needs some working on it though."

"You could attend to that for me," she sighed, rubbing her leg against his and reaching for his hand again. "This place needs a man's hand on it. A girl can't bring it to its full potential. I'm sure you could do it."

Even as the eager-to-be-loved-and-wanted woman said the words, Stella's other side tried to object. Normally nothing could have forced such a confession from her. While not being interested in politics, except as an adjunct to controlling a business, Stella was as rampant a feminist as the staunchest member of the fast-growing women's suffrage movement, and believed anything a man could do lay well within her powers of bettering.

Listening to Stella, Dusty wondered if this could be the woman mentioned by Murat's anonymous correspondent. Nothing about Stella suggested the cold, planning, unscrupulous woman Dusty expected to find. In fact, she behaved more like a teenage girl feeling the first pangs of puppy-love than a mature woman of twenty-nine. Thinking back to the happenings on the slope, Dusty realized that had been the first time she had ever experienced love, or passion, and knew that the reaction to her escape drove her into his arms.

"You still don't know anything about me," he warned.

"We'll have a life-time together to learn," she sighed, then her voice took on a pitiful note. "I need you, Edward. Since I came out here everything has gone wrong. That big storm almost wiped out my herds and I had sunk so much money into the ranch. How my uncle would laugh if he heard. He always told me a woman's place was in the home and that she should not try to understand business. With your help, Edward, I could prove him wrong."

Having seen signs of the big Blue Norther's damage while crossing the Lazy H, Dusty could estimate the losses inflicted by the storm. He felt sorry for the girl, she sounded so lost and helpless.

"I'll do what I can to help," he promised and meant the words; but not in the way Stella's disturbed emotions led her to believe. Any cattleman would have acted in the same manner.

To Stella, the new Stella, the words seemed as certain as a real, down-on-the-knee proposal of marriage. Eagerly she turned her face towards him, eyes glowing.

"I knew you would, Edward. I just knew you would. I'm so happy I could cry."

"Now that's just like a woman," said Dusty, smiling despite his feelings.

"I *am* a woman, Edward," sighed Stella. "I never cared much about it one way or another, but I do now."

Once again her old feminist ego tried to reassert itself. Deep in her subconscious, thoughts stirred and tried to send through a warning. The other side of Stella struggled to ignore the warnings, not wanting anything to spoil her first happiness to come her way in many years.

Wanting to change the subject, Dusty asked a question.

"Is your uncle at the ranch now?"

Maybe Murat's correspondent mixed his facts and blamed Stella, when the uncle controlled the ranch and gave the orders.

"Dear Uncle George?" Stella replied, and her voice took on almost its old note of bitter hatred. "He died——." Her voice trailed off and she rode for a time in silence as emotions warred inside her, at last she turned her face to Dusty and began to speak hurriedly. "No, I won't conceal anything from you. My Uncle George committed suicide after he almost ruined my father's business in the East."

"That's tough," Dusty answered.

"Tough!" Stella spat out, the feminist almost regaining control. "It was tragic. I watched him mishandle a prosperous business, ruin it. I could have saved it even then, but for that idiotic prejudice which insists women have no place in anything but a home."

"You seem to have come out of it pretty well fixed," Dusty pointed out.

"Through no fault of Uncle George's. My father left Harry, he's my brother, and I a trust fund. I'd invested my share of it wisely and sunk almost every penny I possessed into this ranch. The cattle business offered me my chance, Edward. I could recoup my losses and prove I was capable of running a business. And then that storm came——"

'Sure,'' Dusty said sympathetically. He had seen so many Eastern financiers try to crash the Western cattle market for a quick profit. Only a few of the attempts met with any success.

"But I'm working on a plan to clear myself, Edward," she told him. "With your help, I can put it through."

## CHAPTER TWELVE

## That's Danny Fog's Brother!

"Just how do you figure to do that?" Dusty asked. "It'll take years for you to build up your herds again, and plenty of money."

"Money, yes, but not years," Stella answered.

"If you're figuring to buy stock in Texas, forget it," warned Dusty, wanting to save the girl from worse disappointment. "Cattle bring too high a price at the railheads for a man to part with more than a handful at a time."

"I'll get the cattle."

"Down in Mexico?"

"Why there?" asked Stella.

"The *haciolderos* down there have plenty of cattle and a poor market. A man can pick up large numbers of cattle at a reasonable price, if he wants to take the risks."

"What risks?"

"There's not much law south of the border, and none that a *Yangui del Norte*, an American, can rely on. The army's run by *bandidos* promoted for their services during Juarez's war with the French, and the generals use their men just like they used their cut-throat gangs. Taking cash money, the only way the *haciolderos* will deal down there, would bring every money-hungry cuss in a hundred square miles on you. If your men fought through and bought the cattle, they'd still have to drive the herd out again."

"How about the ranches nearer the border?"

"Sold out all their surplus stock years ago, and know how to hold out for a price that doesn't leave much profit margin."

Stella's eyes took on a calculating glint as she looked Dusty up and down. Only this time she did not look at him as a prospective lover. Her eyes noted that he wore costly clothing, even though it showed signs of hard usage. The saddle cost good money, as did his high-heeled, fancy-stitched boots. Nor was the horse he sat on the usual type a drifting cowhand owned, but a finely-raised animal. A western woman would have noticed the way Dusty wore his guns, reading the signs from that Gaylin belt; studied the gelding's brand; drawn significance from the fact that the small Texan's saddle carried no bedroll. Although shrewd in many matters, Stella ignored such vital details. She became aware that he was not the giant she first imagined, but still knew mere inches did not account for the full man.

From the way he spoke, 'Edward' had given the cattle business much study. His voice was that of an educated man, one who knew the Western cattle business from top to bottom. While that filled the new Stella with joy, it also roused the feminist's interest. She could learn much from this stranger who came so dramaticaly into her life.

"Would it be possible to buy the cattle in Mexico?" she inquired.

"About as possible as filling an inside straight flush on the draw," Dusty answered. "The risks would be enormous."

"It will have to be the other way, then," she sighed. "I plan to make a big killing next year, Edward."

"With cattle?"

"Of course. My plan will give me sufficient capital to go back east and regain control of my father's business. Then I'll prove that a woman can handle a business just as well as can any man."

"And how do you figure on making the big killing?"

"By selling every head of cattle I own at the Kansas railheads next year."

Dusty could see the one glaring fault in the entire scheme. Forgetting the girl's lack of cattle, she would still have to trail any she owned to Kansas and beat all the other ranchers who had the same idea in mind. The best profits went to the first herds to arrive. Later in the season the price fell as the supply caught up to the demand. Stella could not expect to make a big killing, even if she stripped every head of stock off her range and drove it north the following year.

"How can you be sure that you'll be up there early enough to get the top prices?" he asked after explaining his doubts.

A crafty glint came to Stella's eyes. "Don't worry, Edward, I have it all thought out. Look, here's the house."

Clearly she did not aim to go into more details at that time, so Dusty let the matter slide.

The first sight of the house brought back some of the old Stella, enough to counteract and bring caution to the love-struck new girl. Suddenly she became aware of just how much she had told the stranger. Never had she opened herself to any man. Her brother knew little or nothing of her plans, for, while protecting him and pampering most of his whims, she had no faith in his ability or intelligence. Not even Wigg, who had come as close as any man before Dusty to gaining Stella's confidence, had heard what she planned to do; he knew a little, but not all. Yet she had opened out and told this stranger, even though he saved her life she did not know a thing about him, plenty of her ambitions and aims.

Although her feminine inclinations failed to quell the new submissive feelings, they managed to gain a respite. She would wait until 'Edward' proved himself completely reliable before taking him fully into her confidence. No amount of feminine feelings could halt her desire that 'Edward' should prove acceptable, be true to her and return her love.

Sensing something of the girl's misgivings, Dusty decided not to press the matter further. While interested in the plans she had for making a quick kill, despite her storm-losses, Dusty figured Stella would only tell him about it in her own good time.

So he made no attempt to question her further. Instead he studied the building which formed the headquarters of the Lazy H ranch. To Dusty's range-wise eyes, few of the ranch crew could be out on the range. He heard laughter, talking and other noises from the big bunkhouse, but saw no sign of men handling the chores that needed doing about the place. Four saddled horses stood before the bunkhouse, but he could see no sign of their owners.

"We'll go in and have a meal," Stella said, as they brought their horses to a halt before the house. I'll have somebody take care of your horse, Edward."

"Nope!" Dusty objected. "I always tend to my own horse."

"Very well," she agreed, still submissive and meek. "But come in and have a drink with me first. I want to introduce you to my brother."

Normally Dusty would not have thought of eating until he cared for his horse. For once he decided to leave the horse's welfare until more settled times. He did not know how soon he might be recognized and forced to make a rapid retreat from the Lazy H. If a hurried departure became necessary, Dusty knew he would not be given time to locate and saddle his horse before leaving.

Hanging the horse's reins over the hitching rail, but not tying them, Dusty followed the girl into the house. She led him into the sitting-room and waved him into the most comfortable chair. Before she could speak, the door opened again and her brother entered.

"Who's this?" Howkins asked, eyeing Dusty truculently and suspiciously.

"Edward Marsden," Stella introduced. "Edward, this is my brother, Harry."

Seeing the other made no attempt to acknowledge the introduction, Dusty remained seated and dropped his hat on the small table next to his chair. What he saw of Stella's brother did not impress him. In addition to a naturally unprepossessing appearance to a man like Dusty, Howkins showed the signs of suffering from a severe hangover, which did not improve a normally surly nature.

"What's he doing here?" demanded Howkins, not failing to notice that Dusty sat in the room's best chair and being aware that his sister interviewed most people in her private office.

"He saved my life on the range," Stella answered, her voice taking on a cold and warning note. "He'll be staying here."

"Doing what?"

"Helping me run things."

A mixture of fury, jealousy and disbelief came to Howkins' face. "Him!" he almost screeched. "Why he looks like a saddle b——"

"That's enough, Harry!" Stella shouted. "If you can't behave in Edward's presence, go to your room!"

As always, Howkins knew when to behave in his sister's presence. Letting out an angry hiss, he turned and stamped across the room to the sidepiece, grabbing the whisky decanter and pouring himself a stiff drink. Then he glared at Dusty and a cold, uneasy feeling bit into him.

"You remind me of somebody!" he stated accusingly.

"Folks're always telling me that," Dusty answered. "Gets to where I almost start believing it, boy."

"Don't call me boy!" Howkins yelled and hurled his glass to the floor.

"Harry!" Stella snapped. "That's enough."

Once again her dominant will exerted itself upon her brother. Letting out a muffled curse, the young man swung back to the decanter.

"No more for you!" Stella interrupted. "Go and tell Cheem to come and clear up the mess. And tell Matic to bring in a tray of coffee from the kitchen."

"Sure, sis," Howkins answered sullenly and slouched out of the room.

"I must apologise for his behaviour, Edward," Stella

remarked, turning back to Dusty. "Harry's a wild boy and needs firm handling."

"Likely," Dusty conceded.

Before Dusty could say any more, the door opened and Cheem entered. While crossing the room, Cheem studied Dusty. Although he did not recognise Stella's visitor, Cheem knew what manner of man he faced. There sat one of the real good guns, a member of the magic-handed few who Cheem held in awe. Cheem might have objected to performing such a menial task as cleaning up the broken glass, but he knew better. Since his part in the killing of the Ranger, he knew his life hung by a thread and that the slightest sign of disobedience to Stella Howkins' commands might see the slender strand broken. Looking through the window, he gave Dusty's horse a long glance. The *bayo-coyote*, a dun with a black stripe along its spine, struck no chord in Cheem's memory; although had that been Dusty's big paint stallion outside things might have been different.

"Bring Mr. Marsden a drink, Cheem," Stella ordered.

"Yes'm," came the grudging answer.

"You've got me interested, Stella," Dusty told her as she sat facing him, after giving her order. "How do you plan to make this big killing?"

"I'll tell you when we're alone," she replied.

Before any more could be said, the door opened again and Matic, carrying a loaded tray, entered with Howkins on his heels.

Advancing towards Dusty, Matic studied him and recognition clicked as the gaze went from the small Texan's face down to the turned-forward butts of the Army Colts. Matic's face showed a mixture of suspicion and fear as he dropped the tray.

"That's Danny Fog's brother!" he screeched, right hand clawing at a gun-less hip.

The words might have afforded Danny Fog some pleasure had he been alive to hear them. After all the years he spent as 'Dusty Fog's kid brother,' the position was finally reversed.

Fear more than anything brought about Cheem's speedy reaction to Matic's words. Having poured out the drink, he was coming up behind Dusty to deliver it. Even as the small Texan began to rise, Cheem dropped the glass and lunged forward. Grabbing out, Cheem caught the shoulders of Dusty's calf-skin vest and hauled it down over the back of the chair. The move came so swiftly that Dusty found himself pulled down into his seat again and unable to reach his guns.

Emotions churned in Stella. Fury at Dusty's 'deception' and the fact that she told him so much. Sudden understanding of why his face seemed so familiar burst on her, or rather fought through the section of her reasoning which struggled against accepting that her rescuer, the man she found love for the first time with, bore a strong facial resemblance to the Ranger who caused her so much trouble—and who her brother killed. The last thought brought realization that her plans concerning 'Edward Marsden' were finished. She could never hold him once he learned that her brother murdered his in a brutal manner.

The fury and frustration she felt burst like a flood and directed itself against Dusty.

"Get him!" she screamed.

Even without orders Matic aimed to do just that. Despite the fact that he did not wear a gun, Matic figured that he, with Cheem's help, could handle Dusty. They had size, weight and numbers in their favour, in addition to Cheem preventing their victim from reaching his guns. Matic thought like a gunhand and knew Dusty's reputation in that line. With the small Texan unable to reach his weapons, handling him should have been easy enough. The first detail needing attention was to get Dusty's guns away from him. Moving forward, Matic prepared to snatch away the bone-handled Colts.

However, Matic's ignorance caused him to make a bad mistake. True, Dusty stood second to none in the annals of Texas gun handling, but he did not rely solely on firearms to defend himself. His natural strength had been augmented by certain knowledge passed to him by his uncle's personal servant. Most people believed Tommy Okasi to be Chinese, but he came from the islands of Japan and brought with him the arts of karate and ju-jitsu, at that time all but unknown in the western world. To Dusty, Tommy passed on his secrets and rendered the small Texan fully capable of handling even the biggest men without needing his guns.

Thinking fast, Dusty decided that he must deal with his frontal assailant first. He measured his distance and timed his opening move just right. It proved to be devastating and deadly. Raising his right leg, he suddenly drove it forward and sent the heel of his boot into Matic's groin. A cowhand's boots wore high heels to spike into the ground as an aid to holding a roped animal, so a powerful kick with one brought agony disproportionate to the size of the impact area, especially when driven home with a strong leg's full force.

Caught in a tender area, Matic let out a screech. His forward progress ended and he reeled backwards, holding the injured area and doubling over. In doing so, he impeded Howkins, who sprang forward.

Seeing Matic's trouble, Cheem acted as he thought for the best. His right arm came away from Dusty's shoulder, rose and struck down. Instantly Dusty threw up his bent left arm, parrying the blow with his elbow. On the heels of the block, Dusty slashed his arm upwards and backwards. He used the *uraken*, the back fist of karate and aimed for the one place certain to free him from Cheem's hold in a hurry. The second knuckle of Dusty's clenched hand smashed into Cheem's face, striking the philtrum collection of nerve centres just under the nose. Raw pain ripped into the gunman, agony far worse than anything he had known before. Releasing his hold with the left hand, he stumbled backwards.

"Wigg! Greenwood!" Stella screamed. "Get in here."

Feet thudded in the hall, coming towards the room. Howkins shoved Matic aside and sprang forward as

Dusty dealt with Cheem. Scooping up his hat, Dusty slashed it savagely across Howkins' face and sent the young man reeling to one side. Then the two men, summoned by Stella's shout, burst in. Although each held a gun, they halted and stared as Dusty faced them. The shock of seeing a man so resembling Danny Fog brought them to a standstill. It gave Dusty just the chance he wanted. Knowing that shots would arouse the rest of the ranch he caught up the coffee table and hurled it across the room. Caught by the flying table, Wigg crashed into Greenwood.

Dusty turned, running towards the nearest window. Arms and hat sheltering his face, he hurled himself through, shattering glass and sash in passing. The gelding, startled by the noise, started to swing around. Landing on the porch, Dusty took a leap, hit its surrounding rail-top and went on into the *bayo-coyote's* saddle. Catching up the reins, Dusty rammed his spurs into the horse's flanks and started his mount running.

Led by Stella, the two gunmen and Howkins burst from the house. Although both Wigg and Greenwood fired after Dusty, he had passed the range at which they could hope for anything other than a very lucky hit. However, the shots brought men bursting from the bunkhouse.

"Get after him!" Stella screamed. "Bring him back dead or alive!"

Four of her men raced for the saddled horses, going astride fast and racing the animals in the direction taken by Dusty.

"Who was he?" growled Wigg, thrusting the revolver into his waistband.

"Ed—Danny Fog's brother," Stella replied.

"Danny Fog's bro——," began Greenwood, then his face paled. "That was Dusty Fog!"

"Yes," agreed Stella in a small voice.

"Lord!" Wigg spat out. "Those four had better get him. Come on, Miss Howkins. We have to stop those two cow thieves learning about this."

Holding his horse to a gallop, Dusty sensed rather

than saw the following four men. While he had a good start on them, they rode fresh horses and he sat afork a hard-pushed mount. For all that, he kept his lead at first. A mile fell behind before the men came into range where they considered using their guns might be worthwhile. The leading rider drew his rifle and threw it to his shoulder. Firing from the back of a fast-running horse had never been conducive to accuracy, and the bullets missed. In aiming, the man threw his horse off balance, it stumbled, caught its balance, then slowed, limping badly. Dropping from his saddle, the man looked down, cursed and gave up the chase. He took the horse's reins and turned to lead it back towards the ranch.

On raced the other three, drawing gradually closer to Dusty's flagging gelding. Another mile fell behind them and Dusty swung his horse along a narrow, rock and bush-dotted valley. He hoped to find a place where he could hole up and make a fight.

Suddenly the *bayo-coyote* missed its step on the uneven ground and started to fall. Dusty felt the horse begin to go and kicked his feet from the stirrup irons, then unshipped from the saddle. Even as he landed, his right hand crossed to the left side Colt. He turned as his feet struck the ground, throwing himself forward to land on his stomach facing the approaching men.

One of the trio rode a much better horse than the other two and had drawn well to the front of the chase. Seeing Dusty's gelding go down, the man reined in his mount and jerked the rifle from its saddleboot. At a distance of fifty yards he figured himself to be safe, and so took no particular hurry in bringing up his gun.

Flat on his stomach, elbows resting on the ground and both hands supporting the Colt, Dusty took careful aim. Then he shot the only way he dared under the circumstances. Caught between the eyes by a .44 bullet, the leading Lazy H hand tipped back in his saddle, dropped the rifle and followed it to the ground.

Seeing their companion go down, the other two stopped their horses. They came to a halt some thirty yards beyond where the first man fell; at a distance beyond which even Dusty Fog could rely on making a hit with a revolver, yet which lay well within the range of their rifles.

One of the pair dropped from his saddle, kneeling and taking aim. Suddenly he jerked upwards, the rifle falling from his hand. Dusty watched in amazement as the man spun around and fell. Nor was the second Lazy H hand any less shocked. Being closer than Dusty to the stricken killer, the second man could see the feathered shaft of a buffalo arrow rising from his companion's side. Fear hit the gunhand and he forgot thoughts of following his employer's orders. Desperately he tried to swing his horse around. Again that bowstring twanged and the man screamed as an arrow bit into the flesh of his leg. However, he managed to keep his seat and urged the horse away as fast as it would go.

For almost a minute nothing moved in the valley. Slowly Dusty came to his feet. A slight rustling in the bushes brought his attention to the right side slope of the valley. Rising from cover, a tall young Indian walked towards Dusty. Although carrying a bow with strung arrow, the Indian made no threatening moves.

"Thanks for your help, friend," Dusty said. "Say, I know you. You're Sergeant Iron Leg, chief scout for the Army at Fort Baxter."

"I am one who was called Sergeant Iron Leg," agreed the Indian. "You are Captain Dusty Fog. One who looks like you rode these ranges yesterday."

"Was he all right?" asked Dusty.

"I saw him from a distance. He rode with caution, but not fear."

'What brought you here?"

"I am Kiowa. Had a sister on the reservation. She meet brother of ranch owner when he came to agency with his sister. Like a fool she fall in love with him. Go riding, she not come back. My brothers found her body. Ranch owner's brother is an animal. We took lodge oath that we avenge our sister. Saw you go to ranch and then come out. My brothers followed to help."

"Thanks, Iron Leg," Dusty said.

"You good man, Captain Fog. I hope you are not friend of ranch woman. We took lodge oath that her brother die the death. When we found our sister, old man chief went to ask ranch woman for justice. She had him flogged and driven from her land. When her brother dies, she will watch."

## CHAPTER THIRTEEN

## You've Never Seen Such A Scared Town

"Danny—dead?"

Dusty sat on the horse used by the man he had killed and stared blankly at Mark Counter, the Ysabel Kid and Connie Hooper. After parting from his Kiowa rescuer, he made a fast ride across country, joining the stage trail not far from town and found his two friends waiting by the scrub oak which bore the name board.

"We found two fellers burying his horse," Mark explained. "They wouldn't tell us a thing, but Miss Hooper here came just in time. She told us."

"You've never seen such a scared town, Dusty," the Kid went on. "Folks there run like rabbits if you look at them."

"How did it happen?" asked Dusty, his voice quiet and brittle.

In a voice trembling with emotion, Connie told Dusty how his brother died. Cold fury etched itself on Dusty's face as the details came out.

"And the folks in town let it happen?" he growled.

"They let it happen," agreed the girl.

Shooting out his hand, Mark caught hold of Dusty's arm as the small Texan was about to start the horse moving. "Easy, Dusty. Hear the girl out."

With an effort, Dusty prevented himself charging into the town and venting his fury on its citizens. Connie explained everything, the reason for the town's behaviour—without excusing its citizens—and continuing with the facts she gave to Danny on his arrival. At the end of the story Dusty looked at his friends. "We'd best go into town," he said.

Both Mark and the Kid showed their relief. Knowing Dusty, they figured he could control his feelings sufficiently to prevent him doing something that he might later regret.

"What happened to the *bayo-coyote*?" asked the Kid.

"It took a fall," Dusty answered. "I'll tell you about it later. Reckon you'd best go watch the trail a piece, Lon. Lazy H'll be coming in after me soon."

"I'll see to it," promised the Kid.

"Let them come in," Dusty continued, knowing something of his friend's ways. "As soon as you see something, get back and tell me."

"Yo!" answered the Kid and rode away.

"You and I'll go into town and look around, Mark," Dusty went on, then he looked at the girl. "Reckon you'd best stick with us, Miss Hooper, they'll not be pleased with you for what you've done."

Scared faces watched the two Texans and the girl ride along Main Street and people scattered before them. Doors slammed as businessmen closed their premises.

Dusty and Mark ignored the actions of the citizens, making for the livery barn and entering. A saddled horse stood by one stall, but there was no sign of its owner. While the girl and two cowhands attended to their horses, Connie heard a scuffling sound in the hayloft above them. She opened her mouth to remark on it and saw Dusty shake his head.

"I'll go stay at the hotel, Mark," he said in a carrying voice. "You'd best grab a meal and then head south to gather the rest of the boys."

"Be best," Mark agreed.

On leaving the barn, Connie looked at the Texans. "There was somebody in the loft. And that was Tuttle's horse. He must have heard what you said. If so, he'll go straight out and tell Stella Howkins."

"Reckon he might at that," agreed Dusty.

"Then her men will know where to find you."

"Sure, and we'll know where to find them," Mark told the girl.

"Show us Danny's room, please, Miss Hooper," Dusty requested.

From the appearance, a hurricane had swept through Danny's room. The bed's mattress had been slashed open, its contents strewn on the floor to mingle with the feathers of the pillow. All the furniture had been moved and showed signs of a thorough search.

"They tried to find a report that D——your brother wrote," Connie explained. "But they didn't find it."

"Maybe they didn't know where to look," Dusty replied, his eyes going round the room. He rose and walked across to the window. "Did they open this and look out on the balcony?"

"One of them went to the window, but saw it was fastened and didn't open it."

"They should have."

With that Dusty unfastened and raised the window sash. He knew how his brother thought and guessed that Danny would select an obvious place to hide the book, the kind of place a searcher would overlook as being too obvious. Climbing out on to the balcony, Dusty walked along until he found the book thrown out by Danny. Picking it up, he returned to the room and sat on the bed to read Danny's last report.

"Mark," Dusty said, "Go to the hardware store and see if there's some dynamite for the Lazy H. If there is, fetch it back here—and bring a pick and shovel."

"I'll see to it," Mark answered.

Left alone with Dusty, Connie looked down at him as he sat slumped on the bed.

"Your brother was a brave man," she said. "He died trying to put spirit into this town. If the people had backed him—"

"I'll have something to say to them about that," Dusty said quietly. "Is that Pedro you told me about still in town?"

"He ran out when Kimble brought word about your friends' arrival."

"Now that's a real pity," Dusty said mildly, but his face was anything but mild. "I reckon the banker was the last of her bunch to go."

"She'll be sending her men after you," Connie warned.

"And one way or another we'll be waiting for them," Dusty promised.

Late in the afternoon Greenwood rode into town at the head of a party of around twenty of the Lazy H hired guns. Although Harry Howkins rode in the party, the men took their orders from Greenwood. Stella had not intended that her brother ride with the men, but he, full of himself after his part in removing the Ranger, slipped out of the house while she was busy with her cow thief guests. Reluctantly Matic and Cheem found themselves enrolled in the party.

On the way to town, the party met a scared and fast travelling Tuttle, who passed on the information he overheard in the livery barn. Greenwood decided to take his full party down Main Street in a show of strength, halt them before the hotel and take Dusty Fog as the small Texan came out. While Greenwood doubted that Dusty would send Mark Counter out of town, he figured the odds to be all on his side.

After riding down the silent, deserted street, the Lazy H men came to a halt in a bunch before the hotel. For a moment the horses milled around, then Greenwood raised his voice.

"Cap'n Fog! Miss Howkins wants you to come out to the ranch."

A hush fell over the crowd as the hotel doors opened and Dusty stepped out. Every man noticed that the small Texan's guns lay in their holsters, but the sight gave no great joy, for the men knew how fast he could draw and shoot. At least two, probably more of them, would die before they could throw down on the shape in the hotel doorway.

"Lon!" Dusty called, speaking to somebody flanking the Lazy H men.

Instant a rifle barked, its report followed and almost drowned by a deeper explosion as the bullets struck a freshly-turned patch of earth some distance from the Lazy H party and in the centre of the street. For a moment pandemonium reigned as the hired guns fought to control their horses. Those who had drawn their rifles lost the weapons as the horses reacted violently to the sudden noise.

"That was dynamite," Dusty announced, when the men succeeded in calming down their mounts. There's more of it buried all around you—and two rifles lined on it."

"You figure it's a bluff, make a move," said a deep voice from the other flank to which the shot came.

Every eye swivelled to the ground, spotting numerous freshly-dug spots in the surface of the road. After that, all movement ended. Resistance would be worse than futile, it would bring certain and unpleasant death in its wake.

"What do you want, Fog?" Greenwood asked, a damned sight more confident-sounding than he felt.

"Shed your gunbelts," Dusty answered.

"Count to three for 'em to do it, Dusty," suggested the Kid, in a tone which implied he hoped the order would not be obeyed by the time Dusty reached three.

The count did not prove necessary. Hands reached down, making sure that no move made could be wrongly interpreted. Gunbelts fell like rain on the main street of Moondog until every member of the Lazy H band sat with bare hips. Even Howkins obeyed the command for he had sufficient intelligence to realize the gravity of his position and understood the futility of refusal.

Fear ate into Howkins as he watched his men disarmed. He wished he had stayed at the ranch instead of embarking on this attempt to give his sister further proof that he could stand up for himself.

"Now get down and back away from your horses," Dusty ordered, as the last belt fell. "Do it any way you like."

Ignoring the rifles in their saddle boots, the men obeyed, moving until they stood in a sullen group out in the centre of the street.

"What now?" Greenwood asked.

"I want to know who killed my brother," Dusty replied.

"What brother?" asked Greenwood.

"Take that charge to the left of them, Lon," Dusty said.

"It was——," one of the men began.

Know his probable fate at Stella Howkins' hands if anything happened to her brother, Greenwood sent his hand to the Remington Double Derringer he always carried concealed in a waistband holster. Out flashed the wicked .41 calibre gun and sent a bullet into the speaker. From there Greenwood started to swing the Remington towards Dusty Fog. Greenwood had but half a second left to live.

Faster than the eye could follow, Dusty's hands crossed and the matched Army Colts cleared leather. Long before the Derringer pointed anywhere near its new target, flame lashed from Dusty's gun barrels and Greenwood went pitching backwards into the crowd.

Terror welled up among the men. At any moment they expected the concealed rifles to start cracking, sending bullets into the hidden explosive charges. Hands laid hold of Howkins, Cheem and Matic, shoving them forward and a dozen voices yelled out the information Dusty needed.

"It was them, Cap'n Fog!" one man screamed.

"We wasn't in on it!" howled another.

Croaking in terror, Howkins turned and tried to leap back to the safety of his sister's men, but they, in fear for their lives, caught him and hurled him back towards the hotel porch.

"He did it!" Matic screeched. "It was him who killed

the horse too, he tried to get it out of its stall and couldn't."

"We never knew what he aimed to do," Cheem agreed.

He could have saved his breath for all the notice Dusty took of his words.

Slowly Dusty holstered his Colts and unbuckled his belt. Passing the belt back into the hotel to the waiting girl, he stepped off the porch and walked towards the three scared men.

"So you beat Danny to death," he said softly. "All right, hard men, let's see you do it to me."

His bunched right fist drove deep into Howkins' belly, folding the other up and dropping him to his knees. Pivoting, Dusty ripped a left which pulped Matic's nose and sent the man reeling. Cheem saw his only chance was to attack and sprang forward. Like a pile-driver, Dusty's right elbow drove back, catching Cheem in the body just as the man's arms reached out to clamp around him. Cheem rocked backwards and Dusty turned, kicking him in the stomach. Even as Cheem sprawled backwards, Dusty continued his turn and drove a fist at the side of Howkins' cheek. Never had any man dared to strike Howkins before and the pain brought out all his vicious, spiteful and vindictive nature. It also gave him the spurious courage of a cornered rat. With a screech that was barely human, Howkins flung himself at Dusty. Catching their balance, the other two men also moved forward.

Then began the most savage, brutal fight that Moondog would ever be likely to witness. Despite their fears of what Stella Howkins might do to them, men and women swarmed out of their places of concealment, gathering in the background. Keeping out of the line of fire of Mark and the Kid, the citizens of Moondog stood staring in awe, as one man took on three, all of whom stood taller than him.

Even Mark Counter and the Ysabel Kid, long used to the devastating effects of Tommy Okasi's teachings, felt a touch of awe as they watched Dusty put his lessons into practice. Never had they seen such deadly, concentrated fury in the way Dusty handled himself, as during the murderous fifteen minutes that followed his first attack on Howkins.

With hands and feet blasting at the men, eyes that seemed to see out of the back of his head, Dusty tore into Matic, Cheem and Howkins. Unnerved from the start, the three men were no match for him in his fury. Not all the punishment went one way, but Dusty seemed to be impervious to the blows that landed on him, his iron physique and superb fitness enabling him to take all that the others handed out.

Nose smashed and gushing blood, Howkins saw his chance to run. Matic and Cheem had caught Dusty by the arms and held him between them. Matic screamed through his fist-smashed lips for Howkins to help, but the slim youngster turned to run. The Kid's rifle started to crash, sending dust erupting just ahead of Howkins' feet and driving him back. Screaming in terror, Howkins turned. Then he realized just how vulnerable to attack Dusty appeared to be. Held by one man on either side, Dusty saw Howkins rushing at him. Keeping up enough of a struggle to prevent either Cheem or Matic chancing releasing their hold on his arms, Dusty prepared to handle the situation. With keen eyes, he measured the distance and stayed alert for Howkins' attack. Up lashed Howkins' boot, but Dusty moved even faster. Bringing up his right leg, Dusty hooked his foot around Howkins' kicking leg at the heel. Twisting his hips to the left, Dusty scooped the trapped leg and made Howkins lose his balance. Then Dusty delivered a hard snap kick to the other's groin and Howkins stumbled away in agony. From the groin kick, Dusty brought his leg down in a stamping move which spiked Matic's instep painfully, and made him loosen his hold. With a surging heave, Dusty tore his arm from Matic's grasp and delivered an *uraken* blow, which inflicted further damage to the man's face. Before the amazed Cheem could decide on a course of action, Dusty turned and drove his knee up between the other's legs. Screaming, Cheem dropped to his knees.

Turning, Dusty went for Matic, smashing the man across the street with savage blows, until he hung, a bloody wreck, on the hitching rail of a building facing the hotel. And then Dusty delivered his *coup-de-grace* in a *keriage* upward kick that smashed three of Matic's ribs and dropped the man unconscious.

Dusty spun around and launched himself at Howkins. This was the man who instigated the attack which killed Danny and Dusty's fury burst on the other. Out shot Dusty's hands, dragging the moaning, screaming Howkins erect. Then Dusty beat him to a pulp, smashing his face almost out of human shape. At last Dusty's hands clamped on Howkins' throat, thumbs gouging into flesh. As effortlessly as a nurse carrying a baby, Dusty hauled Howkins across the street and slammed him into the hotel wall. Pure animal instinct caused Howkins to struggle in a desperate, but futile, effort to get free. His bloody ruin of a face darkened and the tongue burst through the smashed lips.

With death seconds from Howkins, Dusty suddenly became aware of what he was doing. Revulsion bit into him and with an exclamation of disgust, he hurled Howkins from him. The battered shape struck the hotel's hitching rail, hung on it for a moment, and slid slowly to the ground.

A low moan to Dusty's left brought him to face the sound. Holding his injured lower regions, Cheem tried to drag himself erect. Dusty jumped forward and drove a *mawashi-geri* turning kick to the side of the man's jaw, with sufficient power to splinter the bone. Cheem pitched sideways, hit the edge of the boardwalk and then collapsed in a limp heap on the ground.

Not a sound came from the watching people as Dusty stood swaying in exhaustion and glaring around him. His shirt had been torn off and his body bore bruises, while his face was bloody. At last Dusty spoke, his voice tired but distinct.

"Take them back to the Lazy H," he ordered. "Tell

Stella Howkins that I'm sending her brother back to her alive, but I'll kill him the next time I see him."

Silently the men moved forward to obey, lifting the four shapes, one dead and three close to it, then carrying them to the waiting horses. During the loading of Dusty's victims, numerous opportunities presented themselves for the swift withdrawal of rifles. None of the men were fool enough to make a try. Death waited as sure as night followed day for any man who made the rash attempt, for two rifles in the hands of skilled men covered their every move. With the dead and injured across the saddles, the remainder mounted and rode slowly out of town.

Not until the Lazy H men had passed beyond rifle range did anybody make a move. Then the people in the crowd gave thought to dispersing. Mark and the Kid emerged from their places of concealment and flanked Dusty, while Connie Hooper stepped out of the hotel. Dusty's gunbelt clutched in her hands and concern on her face.

"None of you make a move!" Dusty barked out and his words brought the departing crowd to an immediate halt.

"You're hurt, Dusty!" gasped the girl—they had come to first name terms while awaiting the Kid's arrival with word that the Lazy H approached town. "Let me clean those cuts on your face."

"It'll have to wait," he replied, taking the gunbelt and slinging it around his waist. Then he faced the waiting crowd.

The citizens of Moondog stood staring at the small, insignificant blond-haired cowhand—only he seemed to be the biggest man present, towering over his two companions and neither of them lacked size.

"My brother came here because you begged for help," Dusty told them. "Danny put his life on the line for you and you hadn't the guts to back him. So he died. The name of the town's all wrong and I aim to see it put right. You!" His finger stabbed out at the bartender of the Blue Bull Saloon, Connie having mentioned

Harvey's skill as an artist, "Take your paint brush and go around town. Paint out the name Moondog and put Yellowdog into its place. Yellowdog, *hombre*. That's what your whole damned town is—it and everybody in it."

Nobody in the crowd replied, but heads hung in shame, for they knew that Dusty spoke the bitter truth.

# CHAPTER FOURTEEN

## Cut His Throat And Bring Me His Ears

Silent as a shadow, the Ysabel Kid drifted on foot through the darkness towards where a glow of light indicated a downstairs room of the Lazy H's main building was occupied. Back there in the night his huge white stallion, without saddle or bridle, stood waiting for his return, or a whistle to signal it to join him fast.

After the dispirited band of gunhands left town, Dusty told the Kid to see them on their way and watch for a second, larger force, which he felt sure Stella would dispatch to avenge her brother. Knowing the dangers of such a mission, the Kid did not bother with refinements like saddle and bridle. Instead he rode like a Comanche Dog Soldier, except that he carried his Winchester instead of a war lance.

On his arrival at the Lazy H buildings, he saw no signs of the avenging party leaving and after a time decided to move nearer. His decision came after seeing several men go from the bunkhouse to the main building and the light appear at a window. Plans must be in the process of discussion and he thought Dusty might be interested to hear them.

It seemed that Stella Howkins did not expect such a visit, for she had no guards out. Unseen and unsuspected, the Kid swung on to the porch and moved silently towards the shattered, lit window. Although drapes hung at it, the Kid could see into the sitting-room. Some eight men and a woman sat around the room, at least the men sat, for the woman stood facing them. The Kid recognized one man as a Mexican *bandido* who specialized in cow stealing. Standing in the shadows at the side of the window, the Kid could hear Stella Howkins speaking.

"Your problem, gentlemen, is not stealing cattle ——" A rustle of movement followed the words and when it died down she went on, "I don't plan to mince words. You steal cattle, but as long as you don't touch Lazy H stock, I'm not bothered. As I said, your problem is not stealing cattle, but selling it without risking putting your neck into a noose."

"Man'd say you called that right, ma'am," one of the assembled men agreed.

Never had Stella showed her self-control as while standing talking with the cow thieves gathered by Greenwood. On seeing the condition in which her brother returned from town her fury had been awful to observe, and, her first inclination had been to send every man of her crew to Moondog with orders to extract a terrible revenge on Dusty Fog. However, at last she controlled herself and held off the attack orders. The means to carry out her plan of a big killing the following year lay at hand. She must not jeopardize the grand scheme by a foolish bid to avenge her brother's stupidity. So she told Wigg to call in the cow thieves and prepared to state her arrangements.

Listening, the Kid could not help admiring the way Stella planned what amounted to a near perfect method for cow thieves to steal cattle and escape the consequences of their actions. The system of bills of sale offered protection unless caught in the very act of stealing, and also left the way clear for Stella to sell her illegally purchased stock on the open market. Certainly the men appeared to be impressed by what they heard and all agreed to deal with her in the future.

"How about that trouble you had this afternoon, ma'am?" asked one of the men.

"It was a personal affair, and has been attended to,"

Stella answered calmly. "One of my hands had been stealing from me. I don't think we need go further into the matter, do you?"

She threw down the gauntlet and every man in the room knew it. At one side, Wigg let his hand fall to the butt of his gun; but the warning proved unnecessary. All the men saw the advantages of trading with Stella and none wished to spoil his chances by crossing her. In fact, every man realized that such an attempt would likely prove fatal.

With a few more details settled, the men were allowed to leave the room and seen on their way to the bunkhouse. Wigg remained with Stella and once alone he spoke soberly.

"The men are running scared, Stella. Dusty Fog's a legend and they don't want to chance facing him."

"We have to teach Moondog a lesson it will never forget," Stella replied, accepting the use of her first name. Since her experience with Dusty, she craved for more loving and Wigg seemed the next most likely choice to supply it. "Not only for allowing Ed—Dusty Fog to half-kill Harry, but so that they don't dare oppose my will again. We must have an open town for the cow thieves to spend their money in."

"You're a smart woman, Stella," grinned Wigg. "Buy the stolen stock, let the thieves spend their money in town and get it back again. But we can't do it unless we get Fog, Counter and the Kid."

"I know," admitted Stella. "Go and fetch Pedro, please."

Patient as any Indian, the Kid waited while Wigg left the room and returned a few minutes later with Pedro on his heels. The big Mexican showed his interest and curiosity as he entered, it being his first visit to Stella's sitting-room.

"You have keys to the hotel, Pedro?" Stella asked without any preliminaries.

"*Si, senorita*. I can get into any room."

"Then I want you to go there, find Ed—Dusty

Fog—Cut his throat and bring me his ears.''

Startled expressions came to Wigg's and Pedro's face at the venom in her voice as she said the last words. Exercising all her will-power, Stella fought to regain her normal tones. She knew she spoke with all the fury of a woman scorned, or tricked, and wanted to correct the impression.

"It will give the town a bigger lesson than merely shooting him," she explained. "And also prove to our men that he is dead."

"But Dusty Fog——," Pedro breathed.

"He's not likely to be sleeping light after the fight he had," Stella pointed out. "Happen you move quiet, you ought to have done it and be done before the other two know you're there."

"That's for sure," Wigg agreed.

"And there will be a thousand dollars for you when you bring me his ears," Stella went on.

Greed glowed in Pedro's eyes. He would willingly take chances for such a sum of money. Knowing his skill at silent movement and having the geography of the hotel in his head, he figured he ought to be able to sneak in and carry out his employer's orders.

There was another reason why he wished to go to the hotel. On hearing of the arrival of Mark Counter and the Ysabel Kid, Pedro went to prevent Connie seeing them. Thinking of that caused him to touch the swollen bruise on his forehead. For a girl, Connie could throw with some accuracy, and the heavy jug she hurled at him across the width of the kitchen prevented his stopping her departure. Pedro fled the town the moment he saw his chances of halting Connie were gone. When he returned that night, he could avenge the insult and injury.

"I'll do it, *senorita*," he told her.

"He'll probably be using the same room as his brother had," Stella said. "I'll give you five hundred dollars for each of his friends that you kill."

"I'll try, *senorita*," Pedro promised and left the room.

For a moment neither Stella nor Wigg spoke, then she

said, "If he gets even Fog, it will put heart into our men."

"They need it, Stella," Wigg answered. "How about you and I going——"

"Not tonight, Walter," she refused. "Not until we have Fog dead and the town on its knees again."

"Then I'll get it done tomorrow," he promised.

"I thought you would," she smiled and next moment was in his arms. "Put the light out."

The Kid saw and heard nothing of what happened next in the room; not from any feeling of delicacy, but because he slipped away to attend to some pressing business which could not be handled anywhere within hearing distance of the house.

Being a cautious man, well-versed in the art of silent murder, Pedro did not intend to follow the trail right into town. He had too much respect for Dusty Fog's intelligence to believe the small Texan would overlook having a watch kept on the Lazy H trail. However, he felt that so close to the ranch, a mere mile from the house, he had no need to risk riding cross-country. Even the fact that his way took him through a steep-walled gorge did not worry him unduly and he entered the area without a qualm.

Suddenly he heard a faint scuffling. Hand stabbing towards his gun, he twisted his head in the direction of the noise. A shape launched itself from the side of the gorge, hurling straight at Pedro. Even as the Mexican's gun left leather, the Ysabel Kid's flying body struck him and bore him from the saddle. In falling, Pedro lost his gun. He landed on the hard soil of the trail, his horse running on and taking the rifle that might have formed Pedro's second line of defence with it. However, Pedro carried a knife and reckoned to be better than fair with it. Coming to his feet, he sent his hand fanning to the knife's hilt and brought out the weapon.

Lunging in to the attack, Pedro caught a glimpse of something gleaming in the Kid's hand. Then he became aware of the other's stance, crouching slightly on the balls of his feet, the knife held centrally and the left hand helping with his balance. By all signs, in addition to his knowledge of the Ysabel Kid, Pedro knew he faced a knife-fighter of some skill.

Pedro's blade ripped across, its spear point driving for the Kid's belly, but he found the blow parried easily by the big bowie knife. A cold shock came to Pedro and he jerked back just in time to avoid the return lash launched by the Kid. The Mexican people might be a nation of knife-fighters, but the Comanche had also long been famed as artists with the short blade and night-fighting experts to boot. Under daylight conditions, Pedro might have stood a better chance against the Kid, but in the dark, he more than met his match.

For all that, the Kid appeared to have difficulty in making his killing slash. Twice Pedro expected to feel the Bowie knife sink into his vitals and barely managed to avoid the ripping blow that slipped through his guard. Round the two men circled, knives licking and curving through the blackness of the night, bodies weaving in a deadly ballet.

In desperation Pedro grabbed with his left hand, hoping to grasp the Kid's knife blade and hold it for long enough to drive home his own weapon. It proved to be a terrible and disastrous mistake. The eleven and a half inch long cutting edge of the blade pointed upwards and Pedro felt it slash into his hand. Pure blind instinct caused him to jerk his hand back and he lost his balance for a vital moment. He saw the Kid's knife coming across in a belly-ripping slash that would lay him wide open should it land. Down went his own weapon in a desperate parry. Too late he saw the blow had been a feint. Up and across came the bowie knife as it changed to a wicked back-hand chop. Sharp as a razor, the concave false edge on the back of the blade ripped across, biting in under Pedro's chin, laying bare his throat as it slashed almost to the bone. Blood spurted from the hideous wound, covering the Kid's hand as Pedro toppled backwards. Only a bubbling gurgle left the Mexican as he fell, for veins, arteries, wind-pipe and vocal cords had been cut in the savage attack.

For a long moment the Kid stood looking down at the twitching shape upon the ground, then a thought struck him. Not a white man's thought, for at that moment the Kid was pure undistilled Comanche Dog Soldier. A low whistle brought his big white stallion to his side. After collecting his rifle from where he left it, the Kid vaulted afork his horse's back. He rode after and caught Pedro's mount, leading it to the body. Dropping to the ground, the Kid began to make his preparations.

Always a light sleeper, Stella Howkins woke and lay for a few second trying to pierce the darkness of the bedroom. She gave no sign of being awake, but lay immobile while trying to decide just what sound disturbed her sleep. Everything seemed normal enough. The noise from the bunkhouse had ended and she heard no further sound. For all that the feeling of some alien presence continued to assail her. Either there was somebody in the room, or had been in it recently. It could not have been Wigg, he left her, after a love-making session, to help keep going the party in the bunkhouse. Her brother would never enter her room without knocking, even if he could walk after the beating given him by Ed—Dusty Fog. While Tuttle, Drager and Kimble roomed in the main house, they slept at the rear with the servants; and in any case, were unlikely to dare enter her sleeping quarters.

However, the feeling refused to leave her. Sitting up quietly, she reached out and located the matches on the bedside table. After lighting the small lamp that stood on the table, she glanced around her room. Everything appeared to be just as she left it on coming to bed. Her clothes lay where she placed them before retiring, the drapes at the window moved gently in the breeze. She always opened the window just before going to bed and the sight did not disturb her. Standing up, she looked around the room. Nothing had changed—then, as she turned to climb back into bed, her eyes went to its second, unused pillow.

Not for a moment did Stella identify the two brownish objects lying upon the snowy white of the

pillow. Then recognition burst upon her and she
screamed out loud.

Tearing her eyes from the pair of human ears on the
pillow, Stella stumbled blindly across the room towards
the door. Even as she started to draw open the door, she
became aware of something leaning against it. Desperately, she tried to close the door again, but the
weight forced it open. Something fell into the room as
the door slid back and Stella's scream rose higher as she
looked down at Pedro's body. It must have been leaning
with its back to the door, for it fell, landing face-up, at
Stella's feet. Her eyes followed it down, unable to tear
themselves away. Not until the body landed did the full
horror become apparent. The bloody patches where the
ears had been were bad enough, but far worse was the
terrible gash, looking like an enormous bloody mouth,
under the chin.

Never had the Kid's considerable talents for silent
movement and finding his way about in the darkness,
been put to such a test, as when he brought Pedro's
body to the Lazy H. It had been his original intention to
merely leave the body in a prominent position in front
of the bunkhouse, but seeing Stella open her bedroom
window before retiring, and recalling the shattered
downstairs window, he decided on a more effective
plan. Mere lust for revenge did not prompt his actions,
although he wanted to show Stella Howkins some of the
terror which her men inflicted on the people of Moondog. The Kid had liked Danny Fog and taught the other
plenty; and the Kid had never been a man to forget old
friendships, or to forgive those who trespassed against
him or his friends.

So he set about the business of taking the body into
the main house. It had not been easy and was not a task
he wished to repeat. Locating Stella's own room upstairs proved fairly simple, his hounddog-keen nose
caught the scent of her perfume with no trouble.
Entering the room and placing the grisly relics on the
unoccupied pillow raised no difficulties. However,
while resting the body against the door he made the

slight noise which awoke Stella.

Halfway down the stairs, the Kid heard Stella's first scream and figured she had found the ears. He darted silently to the ground floor, crossed the sitting-room and, just as he passed through the shattered window, heard more screaming, which told him the woman had opened her bedroom door. Leaving the house, the Kid darted across to the corrals, figuring he had time for further mischief before departing.

Light appeared at the bunkhouse and main building windows. Ignoring the men who burst from the bunkhouse, the Kid opened the first corral's gate. In the corral, startled by the screaming and shouts, the horses moved restlessly. The Kid ran to the second gate, glancing to where men streamed towards the house. Not one of the Lazy H crew thought to look his way and he opened the second gate without being observed. By now the horses were milling around and the Kid knew how to spook them into wild flight. He ran around the rear of the corrals, halting and cupping his hands about his mouth. Loud into the night, the scream of a prowling, hunting cougar burst from the Kid's talented vocal cords.

It was a sound guaranteed to spook any range horse confined in an enclosed space. So it proved. Wild with terror, the horses broke away from the hated sound and in doing so found the open gates. Animal after animal streaked through the gap, heading across the range. Some of the men from the bunkhouse stopped in their rush for the house, turned and raced back in a vain attempt at stopping the spooked horses. They were too late, not a horse remained in either corral. True some horses were lodged in the barn, but the majority fled across the range and would need rounding up in the morning.

Returning to his patiently waiting white stallion, the Kid vaulted to its back and rode away from the Lazy H. He figured that it would be noon at least before Stella Howkins could gather enough horses to send her men into Moondog.

The Kid's guess proved correct. Shortly after noon Stella, her face haggard and showing signs of the terror of the previous night, watched her men mounting the freshly gathered horses. At her side, Wigg laid a hand on her sleeve.

"You'll be all right alone?" he asked, for necessity demanded he take every man of the crew along with him.

"Yes!" the word crackled from her lips. "Kill Ed—Dusty Fog and the other two, wreck the town. Make sure the people there won't dare go against me again."

Wigg glanced at Stella. Studying the expression on her face, he felt concerned and a trifle scared. He had never seen her act or speak in such a manner. Yet he could partially understand her motives. The Lazy H ran Moondog by terror, relying on the people's fear to help with Stella's plans. So the town must be taught a lesson it would never forget.

"I'll see to it," he promised. "Those cow thieves were worried about what happened last night."

"Will they work for me?"

"Said they would before they left this morning. It's lucky that we put their horses in the barn last night. They pulled out early, but said they'd be back as soon as they had anything for us."

"Then we'll need to tame the town," Stella said quietly. "Bring the preacher with you when you come back."

Scooping Stella into his arms, Wigg kissed her, but she stood limp, showing none of the response which came to him as he soothed her the previous night. On releasing Stella, Wigg turned and walked to where one of the men stood holding his horse. Without looking back at Stella, he rode away from the house and the rest of the hired guns followed on his heels.

Not until the men had faded from sight into the distance, did Stella gave a thought to the defenceless state of the ranch. Only her few servants, Mexican peons and Drager, remained on the property, even

Kimble and Tuttle having been taken on the raid. Yet she knew that she had to send every man, or none would have gone. The hired killers knew enough about Dusty Fog, Mark Counter and the Ysabel Kid's reputation to fight shy of tangling with them unless all of the crew took their chances.

Much as she wanted to see how her brother fared, Stella could not force herself to go upstairs. She went into the sitting-room, but could not settle down. The hideous body might be buried, but its memory remained to haunt her. One thought kept recurring; the condition of the body indicated that her orders to Pedro had been overheard. So, too, must have been her arrangements with the cow thieves. That meant the Ysabel Kid must die. So must his two friends. Stella shuddered at the thought for one friend was Edward—no, he was Dusty Fog, the man who half killed her brother.

An hour passed slowly by as Stella paced the room, her thoughts racing wildly and in a manner which alarmed her. From the hall came a low exclamation of surprise, running feet, a low thud. Doctor Drager stumbled into the sitting-room, his face twisted in an expression of agony—and the barbed head of a Kiowa war arrow rising bloodily from the white bosom of his shirt. Even as Drager's body crashed to the floor, Stella saw the dark faced shapes looming behind him. Her mouth opened to scream for help, but this time there was no help to come.

"Your brother killed my sister," said the tallest of the trio. "You had an old man beaten with whips until he was near to death. Now you see the vengeance of the Kiowa."

## CHAPTER FIFTEEN

## There Has To Come A Breaking Point

Dusty Fog was on the hotel porch, his friends flanking him, and looked at the scared-faced delegation of townsmen who stood on the street. Cold anger glowed on Dusty's face as he prepared to answer the demands that he leave town.

"It's too late for that now," he told the citizens of Moondog. "Don't think that telling her how you ran us out will stop Stella Howkins. When her men come, it'll be to teach you folks a lesson and make sure that you don't dare send for outside help again."

"But if you're gone——," a man began.

"It'll make things just that much easier for her men," Mark interrupted. "This's one time you've got to stand and fight, or wish you had."

"And there's Connie Hooper," Dusty went on. "Do any of you reckon Stella Howkins will overlook her sending for the Rangers?"

"Connie could leave with you," suggested another man.

"And that's all the thanks you give her for risking her life by sending those letters?" Dusty lashed back. "She did something none of you had the guts to do and that's all she rates from you. Mister, this town's named right—now."

All the previous afternoon Harvey had worked at renaming every signboard in town, covering up Moondog and substituting Yellowdog in its place. Shame and other emotions showed on the young artist's face as he stepped forward.

"What can we do, Captain Fog?" he asked.

"Fight! Dusty answered simply.

"We're not fighting men here," one of the crowd protested. "None of——"

"Then get the hell off the streets and leave us to do *your* fighting for you," Dusty spat back. "Listen good to me. Take all your families into the church. It's clear of the town. All of you go there, that way you'll be out of our path and we can shoot without worrying about hitting some of you."

"Way I see it," the Kid put in, his voice as mean as a winter-starved bear's growl, "not one of you rates me chancing getting killed by checking who I see. So I give you notice that I'll shoot first and worry about whether it's a Lazy H man after I've hit him."

"We'll do what you say," promised the hardware store owner.

"You'd *better* do it," Dusty replied, and turned on his heel to walk into the hotel. He did not trouble to give the crowd another glance.

For a moment the citizens of Moondog stood undecided, then the full impact of Dusty's words hit them and they turned and scattered like chickens threatened by a hawk. Within fifteen minutes a steady stream of people headed for the church, although not every citizen went.

"You'd best go with the others, Connie," Dusty suggested to the girl who stood pallid-faced and with tightly clenched hands, just inside the hotel's door.

Connie shook her head. "This is my home, Dusty. Nobody's going to drive me out of it."

"It's going to be rough here," Mark warned.

"It's going to be rough for me wherever I go," Connie answered. "Dusty was so right when he said she won't forget what I did."

"And that's the living truth," stated the Kid.

"All right, Connie," smiled Dusty. "When they

come, you get behind the counter in the bar. I'll make my fight from here. How about you two?''

''If they play it the way you reckon they will,'' Mark replied. ''I reckon I'll stay outside, cover the back of the hotel from around the blacksmith's shop.''

''I'll take the other side of the town,'' the Kid went on. ''That way we can slow them up, Dusty.''

During the morning Dusty had spent time just thinking of the forthcoming attack. He followed his usual practice of putting himself in Wigg's place and decided how the other would most likely handle the Lazy H men. From those conclusions, Dusty drew up a plan of campaign and his two friends had sufficient confidence in him to base their strategy on his theories. There could be no calling for outside assistance, for the telegraph operator, a Howkins' man, fled town that morning after smashing his instrument. So the three Texans knew they must stand unaided against the might of the Lazy H. Dusty planned to hold the hotel, but with Mark and the Kid free to roam around outside, the Lazy H men could not concentrate all their efforts against the building.

''We've only one thing in our favour,'' Dusty remarked. ''Those Lazy H bunch are hired guns, they won't stick if the going gets real rough.''

A faint, weak smile came to Connie's face. ''You're only saying that to make me feel better.''

''Nope, I'm saying it to make *me* feel better,'' Dusty answered.

''Reckon anybody in town'll help us, Dusty?'' asked the Kid.

''I don't know,'' Dusty admitted. ''There has to come a breaking point when they can't stand any more rough-handling and start to fight back.''

''Will it come in time?'' asked Connie.

''If I knew that, I'd tell you,'' Dusty said. ''Let's grab a meal while we can. Then I reckon you pair had best go outside.''

''Trust you to stay with a pretty gal,'' grinned Mark.

"Especially when she can cook, too."

"Don't you think of anything but girls?" Connie inquired.

"Never have since I learned they weren't boys," Mark told her. "I——"

Mark's profound observations on the subject were never to be uttered, for a sound brought all the men turning with hands reaching towards their guns. Then they relaxed for Harvey entered the room.

"Almost everybody in town's gone to the church," he said. "Where do you want me to be?"

"You mean you want to stay here?" asked Dusty.

"I'm not leaving Connie, that's for sure."

Next moment Connie was in the young artist's arms kissing him and muttering incoherent words.

"Land-sakes," grunted Mark. "And *she* talks about *me*."

"Let's go see what we can do about stopping up the rear of the building," Dusty replied. "I want to make sure that they'll have trouble getting in the rear, especially with you watching them, Mark. And anyways, I don't figure Connie wants us around for a spell."

Once again Dusty's ability to think as the other man showed success. Wigg halted his party as soon as they came within sight of the town and gave his orders. Taking ten of the men, Tuttle was to ride to the right and scatter his party parallel to Main Street, then have them move in with the hotel as their objective. Another ten men would follow Kimble to the left. The remainder of the group, under Wigg's leadership, were to charge along Main Street, shooting up the buildings and raising a ruckus to cover the approach of the flanking sections. In that was Wigg hoped to take the three Texans by surprise. During the previous night, while calming Stella's near-hysterical reaction to finding Pedro's body, the matter of who sent for the Rangers came up and Wigg decided that Connie Hooper must be the guilty party. In which case, she would have made herself known to

Dusty Fog and, if Wigg knew Southern-raised men, the Rio Hondo gun wizard and his two friends were certain to be on hand to protect her.

While neither Kimble nor Tuttle cared for their part in the affair, they had no choice but to obey. Each knew that death waited for him should he try to back out. Gripping the ten-gauge shotgun which lay across his knees, Tuttle led his party away from the main group and headed for the rear of the hotel, swinging out well clear of the scattered buildings of the town. When all his men were in position, he gave the signal to dismount and advance.

Much to his surprise, Mark found John Weaver working in the forge when he arrived to take up his fighting position. Mark studied his surroundings and found them satisfactory for his purpose. The forge stood under a shelter, open on all sides except for the roof's stout supports. Large double gates, always open, faced the rear of the hotel from a distance of a hundred yards and offered a wide, clear field of fire. There were several good positions where a defending man might take cover and shoot at anybody who went for the rear of the building and the rest of the area had a high wooden wall around it, hiding the forge from view. Mark figured he ought to be able to make a pretty good fight from there, especially if——

"Did you stay to fight?" he asked.

"No. I've work to do and intend to do it."

"I aim to make my fight from here," Mark stated, leaning his rifle against one of the building's supports.

"That's for you to decide," answered Weaver.

"The Lazy H won't take to me being here. If I was you, I'd either side me, or throw me out."

Studying Mark's expensive, somewhat dandy clothes, Weaver shook his head. "That's where you and I differ. With my strength, I might easily kill, or seriously hurt a man should I raise my hand against him."

"Way I see it, any man who picks a fight with a feller

your size asks to get hurt,'' Mark replied.

"You don't understand my problem.''

At that moment, before Mark could reply, hooves drummed, growing louder as unseen horsemen thundered into Moondog's Main Street. Guns began to roar and glass shattered.

"Do *you* understand your problem?'' asked Mark.

Neither man spoke for a few seconds. Then they heard footsteps approaching beyond the wall. Mark let out a low-growled curse as he realized the approaching men would go along the rear wall and not come under his gun if they followed the orders being called by one of their number.

"Cut across to the Baines house, we'll bust it up and then make for the hotel,'' came the banker's voice.

Stepping forward, Mark halted by the anvil. He gripped the iron mass at either end and lifted it from its place. With Weaver watching in open-mouthed amazement, Mark moved towards the wall. While the blacksmith knew he could equal Mark's feat of lifting the anvil, he knew he could not duplicate what the blond giant did next. Suddenly Weaver became aware that the man he dismissed as a dandy had strength exceeding his own and so knew the problems facing him; and was also a fighter who did not fear to use that strength in his defence.

With a tremendous surge, every muscle giving its share in the effort, Mark raised the anvil and hurled it straight at the section of the fence where noise told that men passed. Even as Mark staggered, momentarily drained of strength by his effort, the anvil crashed into the wall and smashed down a section. Three Lazy H men, rifles in hand and passing the section, caught the full impact. One went down screaming as the anvil landed on him, the other two went staggering and out of control of themselves.

In the lead of the men, Tuttle missed the sudden attack and although startled, recovered fast. Whirling around, he saw the destruction and the chance it gave him. Mark also saw it, recognizing the danger to himself. He realized he had called the play wrong and death was the prize for such an action under those conditions. In throwing the anvil, he hoped to take out all the passing party, but missed one.

At that moment John Weaver reached his breaking point. He saw the banker, Stella Howkins' main tool in holding down the town, took in the lifting shotgun, remembered the Ranger who gave his life for the town, and acted. Up swung his brawny right arm, hurling the heavy hammer forward. As if drawn by a magnet, the hammer flew through the air. Tuttle saw his danger too late. Although he tried to deflect the missile, he failed, and it crashed into his forehead with a sickening thud.

Given a moment in which to regain control of himself, Mark took a fresh hand in the game. One of the Lazy H men had recovered from his shock and started to raise his rifle. Like a flash Mark's right hand dipped, the Army Colt flowing from leather and roaring in his big palm. Caught between the eyes by a .44 bullet, the gunman pitched over backwards, his rifle dropping from his hands, and joined Tuttle on the ground. The last uninjured man took one look at his wounded and dead companions, swung on his heels and ran for his life.

"I never raised my hand in anger to a man before," Weaver said in a hushed voice, as he looked at Tuttle's sprawled-out body.

Following the direction of Weaver's gaze, Mark glanced at the blood and brains which oozed from the banker's shattered skull and nodded grimly. "You sure made a hell of a good start," he remarked. "Only now you've got to fight."

"There comes a time when every man must fight, if he wants to stay a man," answered Weaver and darted forward to collect the gunman's dropped rifle. "What shall I do?"

"Find cover and throw lead at every Lazy H son you see," Mark answered. "Let's give 'em hell, John."

"Just like they've given the town," Weaver agreed.

Having failed to find such a good spot for defence as

Mark located, the Kid found himself being driven back by the advance of Kimble's men. Darting from cover to cover, the Kid turned his gaze to the livery barn. Its corrals were empty, Bescaby having driven off all his stock that morning, to keep them out of the way of flying lead. The corrals offered no cover with enemies on both sides, but the Kid reckoned that if he once entered the building, he ought to be able to make his presence felt on both sides. Only one thing remained to be accomplished, entering the building. Unless the Kid missed his guess, Bescaby had locked up the premises before going to church. The Kid reckoned he would not have time to start trying to pick open or otherwise force entry through the door.

Turning, the Kid sent lead screaming at the advancing men, firing as fast as he could work the rifle's lever and change his point of aim. One man went down, another stumbled with a bullet-busted shoulder before the rest hunted cover. Instantly the Kid turned, ran forward and hurled himself through the building's side window. He lit down rolling, his rifle slanting towards the man who rose from one of the stalls.

"What in hell are you doing here?" the Kid growled, showing considerable self-restraint in that he did not shoot before speaking.

"One of my mares was foaling down." Bescaby replied. "She's just finished. I couldn't leave her."

The Kid rose, looking around him. Apart from the occasional bullet which came through the front of the building, the men on Main Street showed no sign of entering the barn. Springing towards the window, the Kid cut down on one of Kimble's advancing groups, then lead from the other side drove him back. However, the men showed too much respect for the Kid's rifle to try rushing him. From where he stood, the Kid effectively separated Kimble's party from the main Lazy H body.

"Bescaby!" yelled Kimble's voice. "If you are in there, lay hold of that black dressed breed for us, or we'll burn the place down."

Turning, the Kid watched Bescaby walking towards

him. The livery barn owner's face showed a mixture of emotions as he clenched one fist. "I have to do something," he stated.

From their cover, Kimble and three of his men heard the thud of a blow and a cry of pain. The Kid's rifle jerked into the air, fired a shot and then fell out of sight once more. Grinning savagely, Kimble pointed to the barn and ordered his men to move in before the Kid recovered.

Guns in hand, the three gunmen darted forward. Not one of them doubted but that Bescaby obeyed the orders. The barn's rear door opened and the three men saw Bescaby standing at it, behind him, sprawled upon the floor, lay the Ysabel Kid.

"It's good for you that you got him," remarked the leading man as they walked by Bescaby. "We'd——"

Suddenly the Kid rolled over, his old Dragoon Colt lifting and bellowing. The force of its bullet on striking the leading gunman's chest threw him backwards into his companions. Nor did they have time to recover. Bescaby kicked shut the door and sprang on to the trio. The body shot to one side and Bescaby beat down the other pair's weapons then tore into them with his bare hands, striking as he once hit in the prize-ring. Neither man, even had they been prepared for such an attack, stood a chance against the fury of the attack. While fists beat the men around the barn, the Kid sprang forward, grabbed his rifle and used it to hold back the rush of the rest of Kimble's party.

Once more Kimble threw himself into cover, and missed death by scant inches as one of the Kid's bullets tore his hat from his head. He guessed that Bescaby had tricked him, with the Kid's assistance, and fury filled him. Yet too much open ground separated him from the barn and crossing it in the face of the Ysabel Kid's rifle would be certain death. Turning to study the situation, Kimble saw the church and, using his knowledge of the citizens of Moondog, guessed where they would be.

"Get up the church," he yelled. "Drive all the folks out and in front of you. Move it, damn you!"

The group of gunmen nearest to the church turned to obey. Running forward, their leader saw a shape appear at one of the building's windows. Without waiting to learn more about the identity of the watcher, the man threw up his rifle and fired. He saw the shape lurch back and heard a thin, boy's scream of pain. Next moment a moaning cry arose from inside the church. Louder it rolled, growing more ominous by the minute. The trio of gunmen skidded to a halt and stared as the church's doors burst open, a distraught-looking woman came out first, advancing towards them, then the preacher appeared, followed by the rest of the citizens. Only they were not coming mildly.

Even as the leader of the gunmen, the one who fired, began to reline his rifle, a shot cracked from the livery barn and he dropped. An instant later, even as the man dropped and his companions turned to run, Kimble exposed himself briefly to the Kid and paid for his folly in the appropriate manner. The Kid had not been in time to prevent the killing of a boy who incautiously showed himself at the church window, but he extracted a swift revenge before taking Kimble out of the game.

Seeing their leader go down, and recognizing the menace of the enraged townspeople, the remaining members of the raiding party broke and fled for their horses.

Five men lay dead before the hotel, victims of Dusty Fog's carbine and matched Colts. He fought alone, for when it came to the final push Harvey could not make himself shoot at another human being. Now the young artist stood at the bar, the unfired shotgun in his hands and his face pale under its tan. Behind the bar, Connie stood rigid and unmoving, realizing for the first time the full horror and impact of sudden, violent death. At last she could understand why Harvey could not shoot and tolerance began to grow in her.

A series of crashes warned Dusty that men tried to smash their way into the building by the dining-room windows but also that the shutters held. He could not make a move against the men without exposing himself to the guns across the street and knew that somehow he must find time to reload his carbine ready to meet the attack when it was launched from the dining-room across the hall.

Too late Dusty saw the shape appear at the upstairs window of the building across the street. Instinctively he started to draw back and threw up his left-hand Colt. Flame spouted from the rifle across the street, its bullet smashing into the window frame and sending splinters flying into Dusty's face. Pain ripped into him and his eyes became misted over with tears as he stumbled backwards, his left-hand Colt falling from his fingers as he reached towards his face.

Having given one of his men orders, Wigg sprang forward to the bar's window as soon as the shot crashed out. His men refused to take further chances against the Rio Hondo gun wizard and so he knew he must kill the small Texan himself. Appearing at the shattered window, Wigg saw Dusty staggering blindly backwards, caught a glimpse of Harvey and the girl at the bar, and ignored them as a factor. The fact that only Dusty's carbine and Colts had been used in defence of the hotel confirmed to Wigg that Harvey, although armed with a shotgun, refused to fight.

Through eyes half-blind with tears, Dusty saw Wigg loom at the window—although he could not recognize the boss of the Lazy H killers. Without needing conscious thought, Dusty flung himself backwards and fired, but knew he missed. Flame gushed from the hazy shape and Dusty felt the slap of a close-passing bullet. He knew Wigg would not miss a second time.

Connie screamed and her scream seemed to put life into Harvey's limbs. In a single flash, Harvey realized that all standing between Connie and the Lazy H men was the *big* man from the Rio Hondo. Dusty Fog could have rode out of town that morning, kept going to safety, but he stayed; he and his friends, stayed to fight and prevent the Lazy H from having all its own way in the destruction of the town. Harvey never remembered raising and firing the shotgun, but it bellowed and nine buckshot balls tore into Wigg's chest even as the gun-man tried to correct his aim at Dusty.

More feet sounded as the gunmen started to rush for-ward. Wiping clear his eyes, and bitterly conscious of the fact that only two bullets remained unfired in his Colts, Dusty lurched towards the window. Before he could shoot, he saw the Lazy H men come to a wavering, uncertain halt, staring along the street. Then Dusty became aware of a low, ominous rumbling and, peering around carefully, saw the citizens of the town swinging on to Main Street and advancing towards the hotel.

On seeing the damage wreaked during the early stages of the attack, the angry rumble of the crowd grew even louder. The hired killers read grim determination on the faces of the advancing crowd and, if anything, it was augmented by the fact that the people came unarmed. Without guns they might be, but that advancing crowd meant to press on with their purpose to the bitter end.

One of the hired killers dropped his gun, turned and ran towards his horse. Man after man discarded his weapons and followed the lead. Maybe Wigg could have held them together, but he lay dead, blood still oozing from nine holes in his body. Left leaderless, disheart-ened by Dusty's accurately-shot defence, the gunmen turned their horses and fled.

Not until then did Dusty find time to turn to the bar. "Thanks, Harvey," he said.

"I feel I'll never be clean again," replied the artist.

"You will, darling," Connie gasped. "You will. I'll go wherever you want and help you forget."

"You will?" gasped Harvey.

Dusty left them together and walked across the room. Climbing through the window, he looked towards the crowd which came to a halt in the street, standing in much the same place that they stood in the morning. For a moment none of them spoke, then the man who suggested Dusty, his friends and Connie left town, stepped forward.

"We owe you an apology, Captain Fog," he said.

"And we can never repay what we failed to give your brother."

"You came through in the end," Dusty replied. "Reckon Danny'd be pleased to know that."

"It was just his lead that started us," the man admitted. "He showed us that even one man with courage could stand up against the Lazy H. If we'd——"

"Forget it," Dusty said quietly. "I'm going to the Lazy H to bring Stella Howkins in as soon as I can get my horse. You folks stay here and start cleaning up." His eyes went to one of the freshly-painted signboards which bore the new name for the town. "Reckon Harvey can alter them to the old name again."

A low mumble went up amongst the people as they conferred with each other. At last the preacher stepped forward. "I think we'll leave the name as it stands. There may come another time when we need to have courage and seeing 'Yellowdog' will help us remember."

## CHAPTER SIXTEEN

## She Saw Her Brother Skinned Alive

Towards dusk Dusty Fog, Mark Counter, the Ysabel Kid, Bescaby, Weaver, Harvey and Connie rode towards the Lazy H house. Although they took precautions, they found the house deserted. Such of the fleeing gunmen who returned to the house, had stayed only long enough to collect their belongings and such loot as came readily to hand before riding off into the West.

"Kiowa war arrow," remarked the Kid, kneeling by Drager's body. For once his Indian-dark face came close to showing emotion. "They've got Stella Howkins, unless they kill her—I hope they killed her."

A search of the house failed to produce Stella's body, and on reaching the bunkhouse, they found Cheem and Matic, still bed-ridden from Dusty's beating. Deserted and neglected by their friends, the two men showed eagerness to talk. All the servants had fled, but neither knew what happened to Stella.

"Heard her scream once," Cheem stated. "Then she started again, over to the West there. Lord I've never heard a woman scream like that. All the devils in hell might've been at her."

"Let's ride," Dusty said.

"Leave the gal behind," the Kid ordered in a low voice.

Dusty accepted his friend's advice and requested that Connie tended to the two wounded men. Leaving Harvey to guard Connie, the other men took to their horses, riding off in search of Stella Howkins.

They found her a mile from the house. Sitting under a
tree, her back pressed hard against the wood. Stella
showed no signs of injury. Clearly the Kiowa had not
touched her in any physical way. However, her face,
pale and rigid, bore an expression of unimaginable
horror and her eyes glared in a terrible, shocking stare
straight ahead of her.

"What'd they do to her?" asked Weaver.

"Nothing," answered the Kid in a flat voice.

"But look at her, man."

"She saw her brother skinned alive," said the Kid.

All eyes turned to his face, but it showed only an in-
scrutable mask of non-expression.

"You mean——?" Dusty began.

"It's a Kiowa way," agreed the Kid. "I'd've told you
about it, but I figured she'd be smart enough to always
keep a few men around the place to stop the Kiowa getting in." He rose and walked towards a clump of
bushes, looking down and even he could not withhold a
slight shudder. "I'll fetch a shovel out here and do the
burying, Dusty. You'd best get the gal to town."

Much as they had cause to hate her, the citizens of
Yellowdog felt pity as they saw Stella Howkins brought
in. With the telegraph key smashed, Weaver offered to
go for medical aid from Carrintown.

Three days went by, days of hard work as the citizens
of Yellowdog set about repairing the damage to their
property. In that time Dusty Fog spent most of his
waking hours with Stella Howkins. She did not
recognize him and alternated between fits of screaming
and moments of almost coherent speech. In the latter
Dusty learned most of her story and her plans. The
arrival of a doctor gave him little help, for the man,
young and freshly qualified from the East, admitted he
knew little about mental ill.

The story of Stella Howkins, pieced together, made
sad telling. Born into a rich businessman's family, she
inherited her father's near-genius in such matters and
might have risen to great heights—but she was a
woman, and in those days a woman's place was in the

home. On her father's death, Stella saw an incompetent uncle ruin the family business. With what she saved from the wreck, she moved West and made what seemed like an ideal purchase. The cattle industry boomed sky-high with fortunes to be made at it; she planned, in the more tolerant West, to rebuild her lost fortune and prove that a woman could organize and run a business. Only she failed to take the weather into account and the big Blue Norther storm wiped out her herds.

Dusty always afterwards blamed that for Stella's downward slide. Possibly the shock, along with the knowledge that she had failed in her first business venture, turned her brain. Using her intelligence and cunning, she started to fight back. She brought in hired killers, set about terrorizing Moondog—possibly the kind of people who lived in the town, first gave her the idea, for she was a keen student of human nature—she planned it both as a means of supplying money for her plans and also to give the cow thieves she hired to build her decimated herds a place to relax without fear of the law.

For the rest, Dusty learned about her proposed big killing in the cattle business. She planned to have her men roaming the ranges, using dynamite to scatter the north-bound trail herds. If enough herds could be scattered, she would build an artifical demand and the following year, using the same tactics, hold back the other ranchers until she had every head possible on the way north. The beef-starved East would pay well for the first herds, and Stella hoped to make her killing.

Now it was over. Stella Howkins would never recover from her shock. Even with the loss of his brother, Dusty could not hate the girl. With his Uncle's permission, he spent three months at the Lazy H, building up a crew and finding a buyer. Most of the money went to reimburse the citizens of Yellowdog, but enough remained for Dusty to send Stella East and arrange that she be cared for and kept in comfort as long as she lived.

Cheem and Matic stood trial for Danny's murder and met the only fate any murderer deserves. Before he died,

Matic told where the three Rangers lay buried and their bodies were brought back to town and placed in the graveyard.

The sale of the ranch and arrangements for Stella's future had been made. Harvey and Connie would take her East and see her welfare. A telegraph message reached Dusty from the Rio Hondo.

"Cousin Red's bringing our herd up trail," Dusty told his friends. "Uncle Devil wants for us to go up the Trail Strip through the Panhandle and join up with it."

"I won't be sorry to go," remarked the Kid. "That soldier from Austin wants me to help him track down the Kiowa who killed Howkins."

"Then we'll leave in the morning," Dusty said. "I can't say that I blame Iron Leg for what he did, and you're one of the few men I know who could find him."

"Be good to see Red again," Mark put in. "This town's too quiet for me."

So next morning Mark and the Kid sat their horses and looked to where Dusty stood by his brother's grave. The paint—fetched from where Dusty left it—moved restlessly at the side of Mark's bloodbay. After a few moments Dusty turned and walked back to his friends. Mounting his horse, he led them towards the north. Behind them lay a town where children played, folks laughed and talked in the streets, a town which no longer stank of fear and suspicion—a town called Yellowdog.